For my grandmothers, Christine and Cedar

One

Beyond the Black Stump

DAISY JOHNSON

Everything Under

VINTAGE

3 5 7 9 10 8 6 4 2

Vintage
20 Vauxhall Bridge Road
London SW1V 2SA

Vintage is part of the Penguin Random House group of companies whose addresses can be found at global.penguinrandomhouse.com

First published by Jonathan Cape in 2018
First published in Vintage in 2019

penguin.co.uk/vintage

A CIP catalogue record for this book is available from the British Library

ISBN 9781784702113

Printed and bound in Great Britain by Clays Ltd, Elcograf S.p.A.

Penguin Random House is committed to a sustainable future for our business, our readers and our planet. This book is made from Forest Stewardship Council® certified paper.

The places we are born come back. They disguise themselves as migraines, stomach aches, insomnia. They are the way we sometimes wake falling, fumbling for the bedside lamp, certain everything we've built has gone in the night. We become strangers to the places we are born. They would not recognise us but we will always recognise them. They are marrow to us; they are bred into us. If we were turned inside out there would be maps cut into the wrong side of our skin. Just so we could find our way back. Except, cut wrong side into my skin are not canals and train tracks and a boat, but always: you.

The Cottage

It is hard, even now, to know where to start. For you memory is not a line but a series of baffling circles, drawing in and then receding. At times I come close to violence. If you were the woman you were sixteen years ago I think I could do it: beat the truth clean out of you. Now it is not possible. You are too old to beat anything out of. The memories flash like broken wine glasses in the dark and then are gone.

There is a degeneration at work. You forget where you have left your shoes when they are on your feet. You look at me five or six times a day and ask who I am or tell me to get out, get out. You want to know how you got here, in my house. I tell you over and over. You forget your name or where the bathroom is. I start keeping clean underwear in the kitchen drawer with the cutlery. When I open the fridge my laptop is in there; the phone, the television remote. You shout for me in the middle of the night and when I come running you ask what I'm doing there. You are not Gretel, you say. My daughter Gretel was wild and beautiful. You are not her.

Some mornings you know exactly who we both are. You get out as many kitchen implements as you can fit on the counter and cook great breakfast feasts, four cloves of garlic in everything, as much cheese as possible. You order me around my own kitchen, tell me to do the washing-up or clean the windows, for god's sake. The decay comes, on these days, slowly. You forget a pan on the stove and burn the pancakes, the sink overflows onto the floor, a word becomes trapped in your mouth and you hack at it, trying and failing to spit it out. I run the bath for you and we go hand in hand up the stairs. These are small moments of peace, almost unbearable.

If I really cared about you I would put you in a home for your own good. Floral curtains, meals at the same time every day, others of your kind. Old people are a species all of their own. If I really still loved you I would have left you where you were, not carted you here, where the days are so short they are barely worth talking about and where we endlessly, excavate, exhume what should remain buried.

Occasionally we find those old words sneaking back in and we are undone by them. It's as if nothing has ever changed, as if time doesn't mean a jot. We have gone back and I am thirteen years old and you are my awful, wonderful, terrifying mother. We live on a boat on the river and we have words that no one else does. We have a whole language all our own. You tell me that you can hear the water effing along; I answer that we are far from any river but that I sometimes hear it too. You tell me you need me to leave, you need some sheesh time. I tell you that you are a harpiedoodle and you grow enraged or laugh so hard you cry.

One night I wake and you are screaming and screaming. I skid along the corridor, knock your door open, put on the light. You are sitting up in the narrow spare bed with the sheets pulled to your chin and your mouth open, weeping.

What is it? What's wrong?

You look at me. The Bonak is here, you say, and for a moment – because it is night and I am only just awake – I feel a rise of sickening panic. I shake it away. Open the wardrobe and show you the empty inside; help you out of bed so we can crouch together and look beneath, stand at the window and peer out into the black.

There's nothing there. You have to sleep now.

It's here, you say. The Bonak is here.

Most of the time you sit stonily in the armchair regarding me. You have a bad case of eczema on your hands that was never there before and you scratch it with your teeth bared. I try to make you comfortable, but – and I remember this about you now – you find comfort an annoyance. You refuse the tea I bring you, won't eat, barely drink. You swat me away when I approach with pillows. Leave it, you're fussing, give it a rest. So I do. I sit at the small wooden table facing you in the armchair and I listen to you talk. You have an aggressive stamina that carries us through whole nights with barely a pause. Occasionally you'll say, I'm going to the bathroom and rise out of your chair like a mourner from the side of a grave, your hands brushing invisible dust from the front of the trousers I lent you. I'm going now, you'll say and approach the stairs with gravitas, turning back to glare at me as if to say that I cannot continue without you, it is not my story and I must wait until you have returned. Halfway up the stairs you tell me that a person has to own their mistakes, live with them. I open one of the notebooks I've bought and write down everything I can remember. Your words are almost peaceful on the page, somehow disarmed.

I've been thinking about the trace of our memories, whether the trace stays the same or changes as we rewrite them over time. If they are stable as houses and cliffs or decay fast and are replaced, overlaid. Everything we remember is passed down, thought over, is never the way that it was in reality. It makes me fraught, restless. I will never really know what happened.

When you are well enough I take you out to the fields. There were sheep here once but now there is only grass so thin the chalk shows through, lumpy hills rising from the ribs of the ground, a thin stream that burps out of the dirt and sidles down the slope. Every couple of days I declare exercise a cure and we march to the top of the hill, stand sweating and puffing at the top, and then cross down to the stream. Only then do you stop complaining. You crouch by the water and drop your hands into its cold rush until you touch the stony bottom. People, you tell me one day, who grow up around water are different to other people.

What do you mean by that? I say. But you won't answer or have forgotten you said anything to begin with. Still, the thought stays with me through the quiet night. That we are determined by our landscape, that our lives are decided by the hills and the rivers and the trees.

You hit a bad mood. You sulk until it gets dark and then rattle through the house trying to find something to drink stronger than water. Where is it? you shout. Where is it? I do not tell you that I emptied the cupboards when I first found you on the river and brought you here and that you will have to do without. You flop into the armchair and glower. I make you toast, which you upend off the plate onto the floor. I find a pack of cards in one of the drawers and you look at me as if I'm mad.

I don't know, I say. What do you want?

You get out of the chair and point at it. I can see your arms shaking with exhaustion or anger. It's not always going to be my fucking turn, you say. I've told you enough. All of that stuff. All of that shit about me. You jab your splayed hand at the chair. It's your turn.

Fine. What do you want to know? I sit in the armchair. It's burning with your leftover heat. You skulk near the wall, pulling at the sleeves of the waxed jacket you've taken to wearing inside.

Tell me how you found me, you say.

I put my head back, hold my hands so tightly together I can feel the blood booming. It is almost a relief to hear you asking.

This is your story – some lies, some fabrications – and this is the story of the man who was not my father and of Marcus, who was, to begin with, Margot – again, hearsay, guesswork – and this story, finally, is – worst of all – mine. This beginning I lay claim to. This is how, a month ago, I found you.

The Hunt

It had been sixteen years since I last saw you, as I was getting on that bus. At the start of the summer the potholes in the track up to the cottage filled with frogspawn but it was nearly halfway through August and nothing much grew there any more. This place was a boat in another life. That month there were seams of damp around all the walls; in the sudden hill-winds the chimney coughed down bird's nests, shards of eggshell, balls of owl pellet. The floor in the tiny kitchen had a slant that rolled a ball from one end to the other. None of the doors quite fitted. I was thirty-two years old and had been there for seven years. In Australia they spoke about being beyond the black stump. In America they called it in the backwoods or past the jerkwater. These were words which meant: I do not want anyone to find me. I understood that this was a trait I had got from you. I understood that you were always trying to bury yourself so deep even I wouldn't unearth you. The apple doesn't fall far from the tree. I was an hour and a half from Oxford, where I worked, on the bus. No one but the postman knew I was here. I was protective of my solitude. I gave it space the way others gave space to their religion or politics; I owed nothing to either of those.

For a living I updated dictionary entries. I had been working on *break* all week. There were index cards spread across the table and some on the floor. The word was tricky and defied simple definition. These were the ones I liked best. They were the same as an earworm, a song that became stuck in your head. Often I would find myself sliding them into sentences where they did not belong. *To decipher a code. To break a note. To interrupt.* I would work my way through the alphabet, and by the time I had reached the end it would have changed, shifted even a little. The memories I had of you were the same. When I was younger I went over and over them, trying to pick out details, specific colours or sounds. Except each time I revisited one it would be slightly different and I'd realise that I couldn't tell what I'd made up and what had really happened. After that I stopped remembering and tried forgetting instead. I was always much more competent at that.

Every few months I rang the hospitals, the morgues, the police stations and asked if anyone had seen you. Twice in the last sixteen years there had been a flurry of possibility: a raided boating community with a woman matching the description I gave; a couple of kids who said they saw a body in the woods but turned out to be lying. I no longer saw you on other women's faces in the street, but ringing morgues had become a habit. Sometimes I thought that I kept doing it to make sure you were not coming back.

That morning I'd been in the office. The air conditioning was turned up so high everyone was in jumpers and scarves, fingerless gloves. Lexicographers are a singular breed. Cold-blooded, slow-thinking, careful with our sentences. At my desk – shuffling index cards – I realised it had been nearly five months since I'd looked for you. The longest gap for a while. I took my phone into the bathroom and called the old places. I had adapted your physical description to allow for passing time. White female, mid-sixties, dark- to grey-haired, five feet one, twelve stone, birthmark on left shoulder, tattoo on ankle.

I was wondering, he said in the last morgue I phoned, if we might get this call.

You always seemed forceful, without end, deathless. I left work early. There were road works at the roundabouts and the bus took a long time to get out of the city. I had never looked much like you but in the reflection of the dirty window I saw you in the angles of my face. Closed my fists over the bar of the seat in front. That evening I would pack a bag, book a rental car, turn off the water. In the morning I would drive to identify your body.

It was dark by the time I got home. I went to turn the light on in the kitchen and found myself afraid – in a way I had not been for years – in case you were standing there. I ran the tap over my hands until the water was steaming. You were shorter than I was, wide around the hips, feet so small you sometimes joked they'd been bound when you were a child. You did not cut your hair, and it was long and dark, coarse at the top. Now and then you'd have me plait it. *Gretel, Gretel, you have fast fingers.* You would laugh. I had not remembered that for a long time. What it felt like to touch your hair. *Can you make a mermaid tail? No, not like that, try again. One more time.*

I tried to work. *Break. To separate into pieces. To make or become inoperative.* I would finally see you again at the morgue in the morning. *Dread* was a word that could be used also to describe flocks of birds taking off into the sky. The mass of birds rose up my throat, flooded out through my cracked jaw. I broke my own rule. There was a bottle of gin wedged between the fridge and the wall. I wrangled it out. Poured a treble into a glass. Raised the glass to you. Your voice talked inside my head, on and on. I couldn't make out the words, only that it was you speaking; the sentences had your inflections, the words were simple and hard. I gritted my teeth around the edge of the glass. I closed my eyes. There was a loud clap and I felt the wind of it on my face. When I looked you were in the low doorway to the yard. You were wearing that old orange dress, pulled tight around your waist, your legs breaking out from the bottom. You were holding your hands out to me and they were full of mud. The river was connected to your left shoulder and widened out behind you. It was the way it was when we lived there: thick, nearly opaque. Except, on the kitchen tiles, I could see the shadows of creatures ducking and diving, swimming. I ran the tap again and held both hands under the hot water. When I looked back you had sidled closer, weed wrapped in the drags of black hair either side of your face, your old-cigarette smell filling the kitchen from top to bottom. I could feel you examining my life. Even in my imagination you were opinionated, critical. You peeled an egg, skinning the shell off the smooth white globe. You chased me with the hose until the ground was so sodden with mud that we fell, were coated as if bulbs just born. You looked at me out of the mouth of my kitchen with the river crashing behind you. *What are you doing?* you said. *Is this where you've ended up? Just effing along.*

I put on my boots, a coat and hat and went out so fast I barely closed the door behind me. There was a crust of light pollution and a sliver-moon. I walked so hard I had to stop after a bit, puffing. When I looked back there was a single square of light from the kitchen window of the cottage. A yellow socket in the hill. I couldn't remember if I was the one who'd left it on.

I'd always understood that the past did not die just because we wanted it to. The past signed to us: clicks and cracks in the night, misspelled words, the jargon of adverts, the bodies that attracted us or did not, the sounds that reminded us of this or that. The past was not a thread trailing behind us but an anchor. That was why I looked for you all those years, Sarah. Not for answers, condolences; not to ply you with guilt or set you up for a fall. But because – a long time ago – you were my mother and you left.

The Hunt

The rental car was red and the hospital seemed to be mostly a long corridor. I walked past entrances to gynaecology, respiratory health, private. It smelled of soup warmed up in the staff microwave, burned toast, bleach. The morgue was three floors down. I lingered outside, not wanting to go in. There was a board with advertisements for dog walkers, free hamster, new bike only £100. The air conditioning was broken, and when people got up from chairs they left sweat stains behind. The orderlies came and went with trolleys, plugged into headphones or talking on their mobiles. I rarely remembered faces or bodies. I thought of words you used to say: hooch, radiant, sludge. What had you smelled like? I put my wrist against my nose. You had been jealous, selfish with your time and space. Even after sixteen years of living without you, even going to see your body I was trying not to step on your toes. An orderly pushed a trolley in through the swing doors and they opened enough for me to see a triangle of the room beyond, the glare of fluorescents.

I'd spoken to the morgue attendant a handful of times on the phone over the years. His sentences were smattered with hesitation and question marks at the end of statements. He was bald, a shiny pate. He said that I looked the way my voice sounded. I was not sure what that meant. I did not look much like you. You had a stone-edged attractiveness that frightened everyone I saw you meet. There were cut-outs of cactuses pinned up on the board. He shrugged when he saw me looking at them.

Something about them, don't you think? They don't need anyone. They store water inside them.

I was not certain how I'd got into the room. There were metal doors set into the walls and the radio on low in the background, a song I did not recognise. He swung one of the doors open and pulled a tray out. There was a blue sheet over the top of you. All of the air was gone. I could see shapes under the sheet: a nose, a hip bone. The feet sticking out at one end looked waxy. There was a tag attached to one of the toes and, on another, a bell.

What's that for? I asked.

He palmed a hand across his scalp. His hands were very clean but there was some food at the corner of his thin mouth. It's unnecessary, he said, a foible really. Before heart monitors it was to make sure the dead were really dead. I retain a sense of tradition.

That must be where dead ringer comes from, I said, and he looked at me the way people sometimes did when I talked like a dictionary. I wanted to tell him about all the beautiful words I'd thought of during the drive for the places we keep our dead: charnel house, ossuary, sepulchre.

Do you want a countdown? Three, two, one? he asked. Some people do.

No.

He pulled back the blue sheet so it rested just below the shoulders. I felt pain in my stomach, along my hairline, a shock of cold. It was you. A second later I saw my mistake. Her hair was – it was true – the same colour as yours and there was something about the lines around her eyes and mouth that brought you to mind, the shape of her forehead. But she did not have your broad nose – the bridge twisted from a break before I was even born – and the birthmark on her shoulder was not the same colour as yours, that almost sickly purple.

Are you sure? He sounded disappointed. They must have had as many lost bodies at the morgue as there used to be in the canal, swollen, rising in the low season. He lifted the sheet at the base to show me the tattoo, but it was new, still a little sore-looking from where the needle had sunk in: an off-centre star, a map of an unidentifiable country. I'd never been certain what yours was and you would not tell me. *Even mothers need to have secrets.*

Yes, I'm sure, I said.

On the way back from the morgue I stopped for petrol and then sat on a wooden picnic bench by the stacks of newspapers and BBQ charcoal. Everything seemed aligned wrong: the metal of car doors shimmering against the hot flow from the motorway. My mouth tasted sour, unwashed. I felt as if the skin had been rubbed off my hands and cheeks. I was exhausted, as if I'd lived that moment ten times over, as if there was never anywhere I was going to end up except for there: at a petrol station in the heat after seeing a dead body that was not you. It was a mistake to ring around looking for you. There were cranks and dials in a person's head that were best left alone. I got the map out of the glove compartment. I thought maybe I'd recognised some of the road signs (written words stuck with me) and looking I realised it was because I was near the stables. I'd thought they would be hours away, an overnight trip, but they were not far, an hour or less. It unnerved me. That all along I had been so close to that place. I bought a bar of chocolate and sat in the car trying to decide what to do. The chocolate melted before I could even open the packet. It did not – the blue sheet pulled back over that face – seem possible to go home.

On a tight corner I almost hit something that came haring across, flat on the road, a slip of colour. My foot mashed the brake down. I bit my tongue, shouted. Certain I'd gone over it. Whatever it was. I got out. It was hot. Too hot for any of it. I squatted to look under the car. When I straightened there was a woman in a purple mackintosh running towards me.

Did you hit my dog? The right side of her face was shrugged down – from a stroke perhaps – and her words were a little unclear. I wanted to drive on but she grabbed my arm. Did you hit my dog?

I don't know, I said.

Her mackintosh was zipped all the way to her chin despite the heat. We looked for the dog together under the car and then in the bushes on either side of the road. She did not call its name only whistled badly and to no effect.

He can't eat anything, she said, he's on a very strict diet. We need to find him before he eats something. He's always running away. She spoke as if we were old friends. He was a runner even when he was a puppy.

A car came round the corner and almost collided with mine, stopped in the middle of the road.

I can't see him. Can I give you a lift somewhere?

But she was gone, pushing through the tough hedge and into the ditch beyond. I could feel the words for gatherings of the dead in my mouth. I was still expecting to find you somewhere, crumpled up, cold to the touch, your feet facing in different directions.

There was a steep, potholed road that went down towards the stables, a double-barred gate which two girls in tight trousers were climbing over and, beyond, a car park. The stables were the last place I ever lived with you, the last room I shared with you. Do you remember how the girls who worked at weekends used to leave their half-drunk bottles of Coca-Cola lined up against the wall, stand with their faces close together; how there were a couple of them we could never tell the difference between? A lot of them had a strange roiling Essex accent that I could never quite understand, lengthened words heavy with extra o's and u's.

At first I just poked around, didn't announce myself. There was a lesson going on in the arena, four kids on fat ponies. The teacher who'd been there at the same time we were was tall with straightened brown hair and long painted fingernails. A voice like a foghorn but fragile, often wearing casts, slings tied around her neck. She wasn't there any more.

I sneaked down the side of the arena. Some of the rungs of the stairs up to the room we had lived in were broken. I remembered that narrow alley between arena and stable block because I would often sit at the top of the steps and watch for you coming, tripping over the rough earth, swearing and grabbing for the wall. I must have known, really, that you would leave, always expected that you wouldn't come home. *You're waiting up for me? That's sweet*, you'd say though your face always said otherwise, closing in around the words like scaffolding.

I went back to the car park. The lesson was finished, and the teacher came over and asked if I had a kid or wanted to learn myself. Fourteen pounds a go. More if it was for me. I told her I'd lived there when I was a teenager but she only looked blank, searched over my shoulder for escape.

We rented the room up there.

She shrugged. They don't do that any more.

Also, I'm interested in lessons for my niece, I said. Can I have a look at the rest of the yard?

I went around the back and up towards the fields. A little way up there was someone bent, working at the ground. I went under the electric fencing and towards her. She was picking up sharp stones and throwing them out of the field.

Help you? She wiped her hand on the back of her trousers. There was a small silver cross around her neck that fell forward each time she moved. She was older than the woman who'd been teaching, her hair losing its orange dye at the parting. I showed her the photo of you.

I'm looking for this woman, she lived here for a couple of years. In the room above the arena.

She wiped her hands a second time. Took it. Peered. Maybe. She held it out towards me, pushing out her lips. I'm not sure

Can you look again?

Above the arena?

In that room. She did some mucking out. There was a girl with her. Her daughter. She was thirteen or so when they first arrived. Didn't go to school. Hung around a lot.

I do.

What?

Yes. She was looking down the rise to the ugly buildings, the square arena and chunky stable block. I remember her. Both of them. Why do you want to know?

I'm her niece. She hasn't seen any family for a long time. She got some money in a will. I need to find her.

She gestured with her square chin, smudged with dirt, and we went down the hill and into the Portakabin kitchen. She leaned against the counter while the kettle boiled. I let her talk about what she remembered of you and of the girl she did not know was me. In the sink there were cups filled with green mould. On the sofa a teenage girl was reading a magazine and drinking Lucozade. There were some things she said that I did not remember though I thought I'd remembered everything about that time. The noise of music that used to come from the room above the arena, how you sometimes taught lessons or drove the horsebox to shows. It unnerved me. Even the history I thought I'd kept was wrong. I knocked my fist against the counter.

She poured the boiling water onto instant coffee granules. We don't have any sugar but there are some Pop-Tarts.

I'm fine. Did you see her again? I said, clipping the cup against my teeth when I went to drink it. After she left? Did she come back? My pulse thudded in my temples.

I don't know.

Maybe?

I could see by the way she was looking at me that my voice was too loud. The girl on the sofa had put down her magazine and was staring.

People come and go. Let me see the photo again. She held it between finger and thumb, careful so as not to bend the edges. Melanie? she said to the girl. Aren't there stables left to clean?

They're done, Melanie said.

Don't just say things if they're not true.

She waited until Melanie was gone and then she gave the photo back. There was a woman a few years ago. I'm not sure. She shook her head.

Go on, I said.

I don't know. It might have been her. She hung around for a couple of hours and no one really noticed. I saw her on my lunch break. She'd wandered out to the field where we just were. When I spoke to her she wasn't quite right.

What do you mean?

She inclined her head as if she didn't want to say. I mean she wasn't quite there. She missed words out, didn't seem to know where she was or what she was doing here. There's an old people's home not far away and I thought maybe she'd come from there so I called the police. Except by the time they got here it was dark and she was gone, and when I rang the home no one was missing anyway. It might not have been her. People get lost, you know. She looked at me. People come and go. It might not even have been the person you're looking for.

As I was driving back along the road away from the stable I saw the dog. Sat on the verge. Not sweet-looking, some kind of mutt, odd features, bald patches. I almost didn't stop, and when I did there was a disagreement, the dog pacing back and forth out of reach, showing me its white gums. Once I got him in the car he seemed merry enough. I watched him in my mirror, sitting upright on the middle seat, looking back at me. *I don't like animals*, you said in my head. As loud as if you were in the passenger seat. *Put that thing back where you found it.*

I don't like dogs much either, I told him, and he closed his eyes as if exhausted by the conversation already.

I drove up and down the road searching for his owner, but there was no sign and no one answered at any of the houses. I was supposed to be on my way back. I was supposed to be at home already and at work the next day.

I kept going until I hit a motorway. The dog made a noise in the back of his throat that was so like a word I nearly hit the brakes. He paced the back seat, lifted his leg and put it back down. I took the next exit. Lights from Little Chef, Burger King, Subway. The dog pissed in the car park of the Travelodge. I was so hungry I bought chips, ate them leaning against the car. I remembered a story I'd heard about a child finding a lizard in her Happy Meal, deep fried. The sort of story I might once have told you to watch you laugh. I watched a couple having an argument in the entrance to the Travelodge, their wide mouths and waving arms. I followed them in and asked how much a room was. Twenty-five pounds, no breakfast but a vending machine at the end of the corridor. I was inside the room before I could think what I might be doing. The smell of petrol through the window. The triangular pattern of yellow and black on the carpet. Someone else's hair in the plughole of the sink.

A creature paddled through the summer-hot air, crawled up the corridors, dug its way through the door to my room and under the duvet, put its head on my pillow. I clenched my eyes shut. There was the smell of its slow, almost-bovine digestion. The mattress was sodden, starting to shred. I opened my eyes again, filled the narrow bath almost to the top, locked the dog out, got in. I must have dozed because when I woke I was underwater. There were blurred magnolia tiles above, the grim metal shower head craning down. I'd tried to sit up but there was a weight on my chest. I watched the air rise from my nose and mouth, pressed my hands down onto the gritty base of the bath, felt that weight holding me down. In the spare white of no-oxygen I'd known what it was. It was what I'd promised I would never think of again. It was what had been there on the river in that final month. The word felt wrong in my mouth. I saw white stars, a terrible cold in my throat.

The weight was gone. I came out choking, the water crashing onto the floor and flooding out beyond the closed door. I sucked in so much air it burned, clambered out and landed hard on my knees. The dog was howling. I put my cheek against the chilly floor and lay there for a long time.

The Cottage

What I always go back to – of course – is how you left me. This is because, you say from your armchair, I am selfish and clingy. You tell me I was always this way. You tell me that on the river I clung to you like a limpet and howled until the trees fell. You are liable to exaggeration. Telling your story seems an act of mining rather than simply recording. At times you listen quietly. At times you interrupt and our two tellings cluster together, overlap.

I don't remember much of what happened on the river. Forgetting is, I think, a form of protection. I know that we left the place we'd been moored since I was born and that Marcus was not with us. I know that we drove the boat down the river and away, moored in a city where the bells chimed the hour. Stayed there for, maybe, a week; no longer. One day when I woke you'd packed a rucksack and a couple of plastic bags. I don't think you even bothered to lock the boat. I understood then we were not going back. I was thirteen years old and everything I'd ever known was on that boat. Everything besides you.

We sat on the first bench we came to and you plaited my hair into a tight, painful braid and then I plaited yours.

As if we were going to war. I could feel you humming beneath your skin, the electricity of pylons or power stations coursing through you. You were small – though now, over sixty, you are even more so – but you let me clamber onto your back and cling there as we walked.

For a couple of months we trawled hostels and B & Bs, people's sofas they were renting for cheap. We never stayed very long. We couldn't afford it. Towards the end we rode the buses, dozing against greasy windows, waking when the driver came to tell us we had to leave.

We were at the stable for three or so years. You'd grown brave, I think, with desperation. We got off a bus and you'd gone knocking on doors. Someone told us the woman who ran the yard sometimes let out the space above the arena, and we'd found the place and asked about the room. I remember the way they looked you over. We were both the worse for wear from a month of little sleep or food. You lit one cigarette from the end of another. You'd been drinking, carrying around a bottle, wiping your hand across your mouth so hard sometimes your lips bled. They let us stay there and in return we mucked out the stables. Sneaked into a nearby gym to shower. You worked the occasional shift at a Greggs, came home with old pasties. The horses cropped the dry grass with their thick yellow teeth. You drank and drank and in the mornings you stumbled around hunting for a hairband that was already in your hair; clicked your fingers as you tried to remember the names of the horses, the children, the days of the week. Occasionally I hid the flask and there would be a fight. How dare you, you would say, how dare you. I drank whatever was in it to stop you from doing the same but you only refilled it, letting the liquid fall in a long, splashing stream. You turned grey overnight. They asked how long we'd be there, but you told them you didn't know. I was not embarrassed by you then. I think I was still somewhat enthralled. You were like a preacher or the leader of a cult. You had a wide ray of power that sucked people in, your small hands moving as you talked.

The last evening we spent together you told me we were going out. I'd never been to a restaurant before. You ordered wine, gave me some and yourself some more. You were heavy around the eyes and wrinkled all across your face, down your neck and on your hands. I don't know where you'd found the dress you were wearing.

When you said happy birthday I looked at you to see if you were joking, and you met my gaze over the edge of your glass.

It's not my birthday.

You rolled your shoulders, not a shrug, more sullen than that. It doesn't matter. It's always someone's birthday, isn't it? There's something I need to talk to you about.

I was only just sixteen. We'd argued often, a few times I hit you or you me. We were a rock and a hard place. Perhaps that was why you left. I don't think you ever believed that family was enough of a tie to hold people to one another. I didn't know what was coming though perhaps I should have. You'd been hinting about it for weeks, talking about men and their apparatus, laughing.

You have to be careful, you said. You don't want to make mistakes that you'll regret. Do you understand?

I nodded though I don't think I did. I didn't know anything about sex then besides the skinny men you sometimes brought back to the room, the noises I heard them make, the silence from you.

You had a condom in your bag and you took it out and showed it to me. Put the wrapper between your teeth and ripped it open. Looked around for something to use, had nothing but the knife you'd been eating your dinner with. The knife did a bad job. I could see a couple of the waiters together by the till watching us. A woman on a table next to ours was staring openly, her fork halfway to her mouth. You seemed oblivious to their gaze. The knife ripped through the rubber.

You get the idea, you said when you were done. You looked for somewhere to put the condom, slid it beneath your plate.

After we'd left the restaurant you took me to a bar with a square dance floor and mirrors on all of the walls, no lock on the bathroom. You told the man behind the bar that I had never had a cocktail and ordered us a row. I didn't drink any because I was afraid we wouldn't be able to find our way back. I stood at one of the tall, wobbly tables. It was sticky. You danced, yelled that I was a prude, switched your hips back and forth, threw your hands up and opened them out as if there was something falling from above you. When you came back over you were damp and smiling.

This dress is so tight, you said. I helped you undo it at the neck. You sighed and rubbed your arms. I need to tell you about Marcus.

I shook my head, yelled over you, told you I didn't want to hear. Whatever it was you were going to say, I didn't want to know.

Are you sure? You seemed suddenly sober, wrapping your rough hands over mine on the table, tapping the side of my face with your fingers. I now wonder if you would have stayed if I'd let you tell me what you needed to tell. I don't know if this is true.

I think, you said as if I wasn't there, that I should have known from the beginning. You spoke about what you'd seen in the water, about bodies in the river and metal traps. You spoke about the Bonak. We made it, you kept saying, don't you understand we made it what it was. I put both hands over my ears until your voice was lost in the hum of music.

At the bus I got on first. When I turned back you were standing on the pavement and when the driver asked if you were coming you said no. Through the eclipsing doors of that bus: your upturned forehead, the powder on your face claggy as limestone, the lipstick barely even on your mouth any more. Your face thinning moon-like until the doors had drawn closed.

For a while after that I just hung around at the stable, and I think they let me because they knew you had gone and I had nowhere else to go. It was one of the mothers – their carefully made-up, concerned faces – who told on me. I was in the system for a while – that's what the other girls I lived with called it – passed around different houses, different foster homes, similar faces. I don't remember much. They asked me about you. More than once. They asked if I had other relatives, anyone who could look after me until I turned eighteen. I said no. They asked if I knew where you were. I said you were dead.

I was in the last foster home until I was old enough to leave. The school I was sent to was ragged, a thousand pupils or more, scaffolding where before there had been a sports hall, dirt instead of a field. A lot of the kids lived in caravans down by the train tracks. I didn't like it and tried to escape at every opportunity. One time I got as far as the river before they caught me. I don't remember what I thought I would do when I got back to the pine-forested place on the river where I'd lived with you. I don't think I had a plan. I think it was only muscle memory that kept me trying to get back there.

It was language – our language – that tripped me up at school. I told one of the teachers I needed sheesh time, shouted at a boy that he was a harpiedoodle. Over all those years you had never told me you were creating a different language, applicable only to that time, to us. You had never warned me. After a while the other students started noticing I spoke with words they didn't know. They mimicked them back at me, getting the sounds wrong, shouting them down corridors or in class. They started calling me the foreigner or the make-up – as in she doesn't want to speak English, she's too good for English she's going to make it up.

I hacked those words that you had given me out, erased them. Lost them over the years so that now – looking back – they feel as foreign in my mouth as they must have done to those other children.

You're like a wild child, one of the girls at school said. Her name was Fran. You're like one of those children kept in cellars. You're like one of those children chained to their potties in cellars and not even taught how to talk.

I stole Fran's careful stash of eyeshadow and necklaces, buried it. I fought with the bigger boys until they bled or we both did. I still remembered then, I think, most of what it had been like to live on the river, and the knowledge of this was strung inside me and along my arms like blinking eyes.

*

Those were the years of trying to find you. At the weekends I'd catch the bus to places I thought you might have gone. Trawl around asking after you. I had the photo I have now and I'd show it to everyone I met. I'd say, She's short, shorter than us; she's got grey hair and grey eyes. It was hard not to see you everywhere. Out of the windows of moving buses, down supermarket aisles, at tables in cafes or pubs, in cars at traffic lights. I saw you walking or running, sitting, talking, laughing with your head tipped forward against your chest. I chased women down the street but they were never you. You had gone without a trace. You were a ghost in my brain, in my stomach. I began to wonder if you had ever really existed at all.

A couple of the girls hung around me, and I think it was because I looked like I was swimming the wrong way up the river and they wanted to see what would happen. Rosie liked to sit next to me in maths and occasionally she'd tell me things: how she'd pierced her own ear; how her sister had nearly set the ping-pong table on fire, where she was going on holiday. She liked to talk about the maths teacher, who was attractive only because he was younger than all the others. She called him shy and listed the things she'd like to do to him after school. Looking back I think maybe she sat next to me because telling me wasn't the same as telling one of the other girls. It was like teaching someone to talk or read. I had never heard the words she used before. I didn't know the language she was talking in. Even now they feel like words only half-translated: fuck, shag, bang, snog, french.

There was a school trip to the Lake District. There were bunk beds, a climbing wall and a pool where we practised capsizing our kayaks and where I started having panic attacks, nose filled with water, the shadows of legs marching towards me, like I was drowning in the river all over again. We also practised kissing. Rosie was there and another girl who I did not know well. We did it before dinner, on the bunk beds or out behind the swimming pool. They had cucumber-tasting mouths. We judged one another harshly: too much tongue, don't wriggle about like that. They had kissed boys before but it was new to me. I thought about it all of the time. Kissing was, I understood, not even the final act. It was a passage leading to somewhere. I thought about you in the restaurant that time, holding the condom. I thought about it so much that sometimes I found myself almost blinded, not hearing anything anyone was saying.

Somewhere in the kissing I started seeing Marcus, emerging out of the centre of their chests like he'd been waiting in there all along. There was something hectic about the feel of it, almost hysterical. The mouths of the other girls were cold, but the Marcus that came out of them was heated through like a brand. Sometimes I'd look down at their hands on my legs and they would be so like his that I'd feel fraught with panic. With my eyes closed anyone could be him. I wanted to ask you if that was something you saw when you kissed people.

After a while it was not good any more. He was there, curled, waiting, eyes closed, barely alive. I'd feel his breath a second behind their own, hear the tick of his anxious tongue against the roof of my mouth. There was something sick inside him, a moss coating his lungs and stomach, filling his veins. It was something from the river. I understood that. When I thought about it I could see movement through glass, a cursory lick of colour. I didn't know what it was, only that it wasn't something I wanted to see more of. I couldn't stand the thought of him pressing out of other people's mouths, pushing his fingers through the brace of their knuckles, worming from their throats. I couldn't stand it and I also couldn't stop thinking about it. I couldn't stop thinking about what it would be like to have sex with a boy, open my eyes and see Marcus looking out of his face. When I told the other girls I didn't want to kiss any more they only shrugged. We're not lesbians, they said.

The Cottage

After I found you on the river and brought you back to the house there is a dream I start having. I am in the basement of the dictionary office where I work. It's windowless and lit only by wide, bowl lights that hang a little too low from the dirty, panelled ceiling. There are metal filing cabinets in rows. Ten or more are filled with words spelled backwards, another ten with words that have, over time, fallen out of use. There are old handprints on the walls, ancient dusty footprints on the floor, a light on in the tiny bathroom cubicle, though no one answers when I knock. Out of interest I look in the B cabinet, flipping through the yellow cards, but it is not there. *Bonak.* Of course it's not; it's not even a real word. It doesn't even exist.

I go down the corridor to the lift. I know I am dreaming because in reality it was refurbished a long time before I started working there, but here it is old, with a cage door that I press into the side and worn red velvet walls. It moves slowly, clanking through the levels. We reach the office floor. There are no phones allowed on desks, and the receiver in one of the two phone booths in the corner is swinging from its hook. I pick it up thinking I will hear your voice, but there is not even a dial tone.

The coffee machine in the kitchen is warm to the touch; the fridge – which I swing open – is full of carefully labelled Tupperware. ARUNDHATI, DO NOT EAT. NAT 13/4/2017. BENJI. On the walls of the corridor are posters for silence. I move into the warren of cubicles. Most of the computers are on, the tidy desks lined with different-coloured citation cards, the trays for incoming and outcoming messages full. I walk towards my desk, but when I get there someone else's things are on it. A red apple with tidy teeth marks, a jar of greenish pickled eggs, an encyclopedia with pages folded down. When I sit in the chair it is uncomfortable, set at a height for a shorter person. I look on the computer for signs of who has stolen my desk. There are emails but they are signed off only, always, with an S. There is a noise somewhere in the office. I stand and look over the tops of the cubicles. The automatic lights at the other end have come on, and – as I watch – go off again. I sit back down and start to read the definitions that are laid out. Some of the words are so crossed out I can read only parts. *The sound of the river at night. A moment of alone time.* Near the bottom of the pile one word is written clearly. *Bonak: what we are afraid of.* Even in a dream seeing it written down drops the bottom of my stomach out. I close my hand over the top of it.

There is the sound of an object falling onto the carpeted floor. I stand and move out into the main corridor between wall and cubicles. The carpet ahead is rucked up as if someone had caught it with the side of their shoe. I push it down flat. Above my head the panelling of the ceiling starts to rattle, shifting out of place to reveal the mess of pipes and wires beyond. I see swift movement. A panel ahead crashes to the floor. More start to fall, breaking as they do or bouncing off desks and spinning away.

With them comes water, not clean, filtered, office water but rank with weeds, torn nets emptying out threshing fish which drown on the carpet. The water falls from the ceiling. There is the sound of something shuttling about above my head, fast, rattling the glass in the windows. I hear it falling to the ground behind me. I do not turn. I listen to it moving across the floor. I know what you are, I think. Except when I wake up I've forgotten again.

The morning after I first have the dream I find you at the table wearing my dressing gown and slippers, eating oranges and hard-boiled eggs, leaving the shells in neat little piles. You've brushed your hair and it lies flat against your head like a swimming cap. You spit a pip into your hand and tell me I was shouting in the night and was this going to be a regular occurrence? Because if it was perhaps I could get a hotel somewhere and let you sleep in peace?

There are, between us, decades of bad feeling, a swamp of miscommunication, missed birthdays, the whole of my twenties, a cut-away breast I was not there to witness going. I think of bringing my hand down across your face the way you occasionally did at the stable. Not hard but with feeling.

You peel me an egg. There's something I remembered, you say.

The front of your dressing gown has edged up and I can see the mouthing scar line where your left breast used to be.

I eat the egg. What did you remember? Something about the winter with Marcus?

You wave your hands impatiently and then wipe them across your mouth. No, no.

OK, what then?

You narrow your eyes at me. You look like someone I have kidnapped from the wild, your dirty fingernails and seal-like hair. I sit and wait. You seem to have more words than you know what to do with. Than I know what to do with. They spill out of you.

Sarah

It begins – I understand now – with you. This – where I wasn't expecting or looking for it – is the story of you and the man who could have been my father.

You were thirty-one. The year was 1978 or thereabouts. Though you did not know it, a spacecraft had set out for Saturn. It would discover that if a body of water big enough could be found then the planet would float in it. The length of a day on Saturn was short, barely ten hours. In the *Oxford English Dictionary* the words *cold-call* and *gridlock* were listed for the first time. The doctor at the surgery you worked at as a receptionist said – flirting, stealing a segment of the orange you'd brought for lunch – that you had child-bearing hips. You simpered, bore the insult. You understood what he meant was that you were not thin. You were small, barely reached his shoulder, but you were not thin. You had a body that could hold up; a bottom that could balance the weight of a rucksack on it and a pair of thighs that were the size of some girls' backs. It was a body – you'd learned – that bred a type of confusion easily turned to your advantage. At school there had been the sporty boys who tasted of sweat and grass stains; the science boys with their fingers and fringes singed; the tall boys and the short ones, the skinny ones and the ones with flesh going spare. Your twenties were – from what you could understand of them – made for men. Mostly they were older. Men who populated the same bars as you did; men who stood in line for taxis, men who carried shopping bags, or paused to tie their laces before getting on to trains, before opening doors for you. Men who liked espressos, steak tartare, white chocolate macaroons; men who enjoyed subtitled films, who wrote in the margins of books then gave them to you to read after you'd had sex in their city flats or cabins in the woods or country houses with corridors like throats leading to doors you walked in and out of. Men who liked thin-strapped bras, who liked black cotton underwear, who liked bedposts and phone boxes and swimming pools.

By the time you met Charlie you were old enough that he was the end of a long list. There had been a bad break-up with a professor who sometimes came into the cafe you worked in. A regally greying professor who, each time you were finished, would sit on the side of the bed and weep. Told you as he was leaving for the last time that he wouldn't come again because you looked like his daughter. Turned at the door and said – face washed clean and mean with tears – that he thought his daughter might be a slut the way you were. That was that. You'd sworn off them. All the different sorts of them: men in suits and ties, men in scrubs and red underwear and socks with days of the week on. Older men in particular who thought you owed them something, a slice of the youth they had wasted.

You got the job at the doctor's because it had seemed – the white walls and ceiling, the carpets stained with age in the corners, the hoover you had to run around every morning and evening, the blue paper sheets that covered the ripped-leather examining tables – a place entirely lacking in lust. Even the doctor – so your type you'd felt your heart sink when he came sashaying in that first day – stealing your bits of orange and offering you snifters from his secret gin supply did nothing to your resolve. Perhaps, you thought, the thirties were the celibate years. A decade at least. The flat you rented had yellow floral wallpaper and other people's stains on the mattress. This was the life of a spinster. You bought Chinese takeaway from the shop underneath your flat, ate it on a bench across the road watching the cars going past. You organised and reorganised the stationery drawer at the surgery: the red loops of masking tape, the staples spilling out of your hands, the teeth of the hole punch pressing down perfect circles.

One morning – already half-mad with boredom – you took a different route to the surgery, slipping down the narrow track beside the bridge, skidding in your heels, walking along the towpath that ran next to the canal. There were ducks in the oily water and boats with rusty doors and flowerpots on their roofs. Halfway down there was a green barge with a man sitting on the back, his legs up, a cup of coffee cooling on the deck next to him. His hands were busily whittling, though you could not see at what. Later you would think of that moment. The boat pulled in close to the weedy, muddied side; long legs bracing his skinny body; the rattle of the train passing on the bridge overhead so that for a moment you could barely hear yourself thinking about him, thinking about him so hard you should have known it would come to no good. You didn't understand what it was about him. He was too skinny and not nearly keen enough. Still. You caught yourself – early morning and evenings too – taking the longer route along the canal. Slower each time you walked past, until one day you stopped and he was looking at you.

The first time you went on the boat it was not the way you imagined. He seemed sometimes not to notice you were there and you wondered if there were other women who came and sat while he moved around. You asked him for tea but when he said he only had whisky drank that instead. You found yourself studying his body. He had an economical look. He hitched often at the waistband of his trousers with both hands as if he'd had bulk he no longer possessed. He spoke in riddles, in codes and secrets. Laughed and laughed. He was whittling, he told you, a lure. A what? He would not explain. Mostly when you went he was cooking. You told him you couldn't even make toast and he sucked the air into the back of his throat, nudged you into place, gave you a knife. He said everything tasted salty because of how much you cut yourself. He sharpened his knives on his belt. Everything was too spicy though you pretended it was not. In your room, when you touched yourself, you burned from your chilli-handed graspings. He taught you – on the long tow-path with the rattle of the train – how to smoke.

You stayed longer and longer. The water and electricity were turned off in your flat. The doctor's office stopped ringing. He did not ask you to stay but most nights his body pressed you down into the mattress and so you did. You heard the rain on the roof of the boat; you heard the train rushing past, you heard the slow slugging of his pulse.

In the days – stirring the great cauldrons of food he made or sunbathing and smoking on the roof – you would often hear something. What was it? Sitting up or putting down the wooden spoon. It was inside you, creaking like an old house moving in westerly winds or a boat lifted on a strong current. Something different from all the others; their beautiful bodies and quiet faces. Something about the shape of his heavy hands, his spine banking through the moss of his skin, the boat beneath him. He told you that he dreamed of going blind, of waking and being able to see nothing but night, of seeing a pin moving with speed towards his pupils. He loved you with all his might, he was different from the others. They were not, after all, the years of celibacy. Perhaps, though, the years of something else.

There had been girls you'd grown up with who'd wanted babies so hard they could barely put it into words – a chemical ache. You had never been that way. You did not consider your body a carrier, an appendage to something else. There had been scares before, small worries, late periods. Except it had never come to anything, and this had only proved to you that you were not capable; you were not built to do it. Some machines were made for cutting or filling or forming something to shape and some were not. You did not have the mechanics for baby-making. More than that – the older you got the more you understood – you did not have the resolve. You were a runner, a giver-upper. It was a pattern laid out behind you like a reversed breadcrumb trail you could have followed – if you'd had the impulse – to prove that you were no one to be depended upon.

Still. He sometimes spoke about the children he'd always dreamed of. You let him. He did not seem to notice your silence. He had wanted them since he was a boy who'd thought he could do better than his parents.

One morning: his excited face, his grateful clever hands, you let him drop the pack of condoms into the canal. You sure? he said over and over. Are you sure? The truth was – his hands beneath the tight elastic of your underwear – that you thought nothing of it. He could want it as much he wanted. Nothing would come of it. You were certain of this. You were simply not built that way.

The baby was there whether you had wished for it or not. And you still believing it was not possible until it was too late to do anything about it. You grew so fast it felt like something wolfing through you, stealing space. You could no longer move with ease through the boat; jump from barge to bank, open the heavy locks. You did not tell him that you had never wanted a child. You would do it, if for nothing else then for him. People did it all the time. People did it daily, thoughtlessly. Couples had babies because it was something made of the two of them. You would have a baby because it was made of a part of him.

Two

Things Go Missing in the Night

The Cottage

The house is different with you here. The scattered cups and periodic emptying of the fridge in the middle of the night. The way you think burrowing into my mind so that I find myself losing days, forgetting the ordering of weeks. The fights I try to avoid but which swim up out of you, last whole nights and end with you weeping in the bath. The obsessions that rush over you. The day you spend making vats of curry, your hands orange with turmeric; too bored or distracted by the time you're finished to eat any of it. The day we spend up by the stream so that you can fish with your hands, crouched for hours in the low, sluggish water while you bend and grasp for fish I cannot see, do not think are there. You become obsessed, also, with thoughts of inevitability, unavoidability. There is a sense of doom about you, dragging your wretched hide around my house. I know, you keep saying, what will happen. And when I quiz you, angrier and angrier by the second, you say only that there is no escaping, that the way we will end up is coded into us from the moment we are born and that any decisions we make are only mirages, ghosts to convince us of free will. And I want to shout that you chose to leave me, no one made you do it, you cannot lie down behind your badly made decisions and call them fate or determinism or god. But sometimes I wonder if you are right and if all of our choices are remnants of all the choices we made before. As if decisions were shards from the bombs of our previous actions. I do not say this to you. I try not to listen when you speak, and I make you tea, and I sleep when you sleep like a mother with a newborn she does not quite yet know how to look after.

I have been thinking about Marcus, and when I ask if you remember first meeting him you say who, and what are you talking about? Except I know from the look in your eyes and the way you sidle away that you do. A fragment has come back to me. I am uncertain what it means and when I recount it you become angry and a window is broken. The man who comes to fix it watches you as if you frighten him. You open and close your jaws with a snap and he jumps.

I ate men like you for breakfast when I was her age, you say and point at me.

I can barely hear what you are saying. The memory lays itself over the dirty house, your clawed hands, the new pane of glass, the man's toolbox open on the table.

I am thirteen years old and indebted to you and to words and to the tangle of bank and water and forest. I believe that nothing is set in stone, that I can change anything I want by catching river rats, frogs, rough grey squirrels, field mice, daddy long-legs, tadpoles. It is nearly the end of the winter that Marcus came – the last winter we were on the river – and I am belly down on the roof of our boat. There is a curl of mist that cuts the trunks off at their knees. The boat is not tied to the bank but in the middle of the river, the mooring ropes drawn tight towards the shore. I hold my head in the crook of my arm, and my breath fogs and then clears the glass in the circle of roof hatch. It is night and the only light is in the boat beneath me. You, I remember, had told me you needed a sheesh, asked me to sleep on the roof. Marcus had been in the boat with you.

At times I am inside myself. I can taste the bark I'd skinned from a tree and chewed until it turned to pulp, can see the crescents of dirt under my fingernails. I look down through the roof hatch.

At other times I am on the bank and I am the age I am with you in my house, bent-toed in my too-small boots, searching for signs of you: cigarette butts, bits of bread, burnt-out matches. From the ground I can only just make out my younger self, hunched forward on the roof, elbows sharding out to either side, intent on watching.

Through the roof hatch something moves. It is double-headed, has more limbs than it must need, flings in and out of the dull pockets of candlelight. I cup my face in my hands, press my nose against the glass as hard as I can, hold my breath. Is it the Bonak?

Each time I come close to understanding what I am seeing I find myself on the bank, tugging at the short hair behind my ears, whistling for a dog long gone, trying to remember the words we need to tell this story.

The man fixing the window says something under his breath and you chase him as far as his car, stand throwing stones as he roars down the track. There is a heat haze over the hills and when you come back to the house there are sweat loops under your arms, across your chest. You tell me you need lemonade. You need a cigarette. You need a deckchair. You need some fucking alone time. I am so frustrated by you. Your pig-headedness. You rile me. You piss me off. You do not belong here.

I need to forget the person you were and instead record who you have become. You do not seem to feel pain. I watch you scald yourself on the kettle and continue as if nothing had happened. You are intensely sensitive to small noises or smells: complain about the wind in the chimney or the water in the pipes, refuse to go into a room after I've cooked. You speak with great, loud authority on anatomy and disease. I do not know if you are making it up or have gathered the knowledge across the years. You tell me I am iron deficient and probably have coeliac disease. You hold my hands and push at the cuticles, make noises I cannot interpret, pull the skin around my eyes down. There is nothing you won't talk about, gain great pleasure from telling me about bowel movements, the colour of your urine, plucking chin hairs. The way you talk about sex is sweeping, generalised. Bodies seep together in your sentences so it is never clear if you are speaking about one event or multiple ones. When you are not talking about Charlie – the man on the boat – the men are submissive, cowed, at times afraid. There is one you speak about with slow regret. Younger, inexperienced, fumblingly nervous. A mistake from the start. Most of the others I think you tell me to be funny; their heads knocking against walls, their flaccidity or the speed with which they orgasm. If I laugh, even a little, you look pleased and take my hand or give me an orange from the fruit bowl.

There is also further degeneration. You shout for me to come, come quickly. When I get there you are holding my big Oxford dictionary open in your hands, wielding it at me.

I know that it's a word, you shout. I know it is, I know it is.

I try and calm you. You are fraught. You throw the book onto the table and it smashes a glass. You tear through the pages so that some are ripped.

I know it is, I know it is.

What? What is the word?

You glare at me, your lips pulled back over the gums, your fingers ridged. The word you were looking for is *egaratise* and it means to disappear yourself, to step out of your past. I tell you there is no such word and show you the place in the dictionary to prove it. You seem frightened, follow me around the house, dogging my heels so that we both nearly fall.

Small words bother you. *Tap, screw, step, handle.* You pronounce them wrong or speak as if they mean something else. *Can you turn the handle on the bath to put more hot in? It's too stiff for me.* Mostly I pretend nothing has happened and you swim on, blithely. I think you do not notice until, one day, I see you in the kitchen, gripping the sink with both hands. You are saying the word *parasitic* over and over again. Now para-SIT-ic. Now PARA-sit-ic. Your left foot knocks out the beat on the floor. At first I do not understand what you are doing but after a moment I realise you are examining your use of the word for flaws, testing yourself for further loss.

You know exactly what is happening to you. No one is as undone by your age as much as you are. All of your ignorance is only for me.

Children are supposed to leave their parents. That's the way it's supposed to be. By the time you're a parent you are supposed to have got over it, whatever it is that sets us rolling. Parents are not supposed to leave their children.

I need to ask you something, I say. Do you think you would mind?

Why would I mind? You shake your head. You seem to have forgotten any of your previous irritation.

You might not remember.

You don't argue with me. You lean against me, companionable but careful. I can feel the gap where your breast had been.

Do you remember, I say, the winter Marcus came?

It's summer now though.

Yes. It was winter then. We were living on the river. Do you remember? I found you there a couple of days ago.

You hummed a little, shook your head, tapped my knee. I forged on. We'd been living there my whole life. Just you and me. But one day a man came. A boy. And he stayed with us. Not for very long, a month at most. There was something in the river, I don't know what. I think we tried to catch it.

Did we?

Yes.

I don't remember that.

Do you remember anything?

You shrug, dig in the pockets of the dressing gown, come up empty. You show me your hands, palms up. I press them down.

Do you remember what happened to Marcus?

You take my hand between yours and rub at it hard, blow into the gap so I feel your clammy breath on my skin. I feel the shock of you touching me. I used to – didn't I? – wrap my arms around your legs and press my face into the curve of your knees. I used to bring you what I'd found in the forest or the water: current-shaped stones, dock leaves, snails that you cooked in garlic and butter. When I was young you held the hose high and we showered together out on the path, your hands working at the knots in my hair like they were puzzles you knew the answer to.

You are suddenly, as if a switch has been pressed, very present. I can see from looking at you that you know everything, that you are full with all the years that have passed and what they've left.

I should have known when he first came, you say. You angle your head. There was something about him. I think I told myself it was lust, a new sort of lust, consuming. There was something familiar about him, like I'd loved him before. I should have known.

The River

There are more beginnings than there are ends to contain them. Somewhere you and the father who is not my father are in a narrow bed, as yet unafraid, long limb to long limb, mouth to mouth as if one of you was dying already. Somewhere I am standing in the dictionary office listening to the phone ring in an empty morgue. Somewhere I am opening the door to the cottage on the hill and you are pushing past me, commenting on the beige wallpaper that has been here as long as I have, the mouldy cornices and lack of ashtrays. *Couldn't you even buy a bloody car?* And somewhere Margot is walking. Here I fall back on imagination, possibility. I fit her words into my cheek and hope she will not mind if I make allowances, embellish. Somewhere she is walking and perhaps she hears me, the echo of repetition and thinks, That's not right. Listen. Listen, this is how it went.

There was a tent in Margot's bag but she was too tired to use it. She crawled as far as she could into the bush. There was a slime of leaves, beer cans cut open, a white-filmed balloon that skidded under her bad leg. Through the hedge she could see the canal, lit by the oil-spill throw of street lights, the surprise exclamation of car headlights rising and then lowering over the bridge. She pulled the hood of her sleeping bag over her head. Towards the tail end of the night some people came and slept further down the path, beneath the bridge and she was woken by their calling to one another. In the first inch of waking she had forgotten. Then it came back to her. She could not sleep after that. There was a crease of frost on the ground and the sleeping bag was wet. She watched the dirty morning descend over the water.

She emptied the bag Fiona had filled for her. It was not without compassion. A bar of chocolate, a bag of bread, some banknotes folded up, half a round of toilet roll and some tampons. The tent had not been used for a long time and was damp-smelling. Something her father had said came back to her though only partly; something about how achieving only the smallest thing was still an achievement. She tried to hear the sound of her body, churning, mechanical, still working despite everything. When she thought about what she was doing she was so afraid she could barely see. She pressed everything back into the bag, straightened, began to walk.

She walked for two hours and then stopped. Dual carriageways passed noisily over the canal and away; old railway tracks broke off mid-air; fields of what might have been crops were sunk beneath a scum of flood water. Occasionally – though less and less – she would swing about, start to head back the way she'd come. It seemed inconceivable to be walking away from home. Her hands stuttered at her pockets, at her thin hair, at her left leg, which was twisted. She closed her eyes, imagined the walls of her parents' house rising around her like a ribcage, the familiar doors swinging closed.

Four fishermen – their tent pegs left in the ground from the night before – were so insistent that she have one of the burgers they were cooking in a dirty frying pan that she squatted next to them, ate the undercooked meat with her hands. Took the second she was offered. They spoke slowly to one another. She barely listened. Not knowing what else to do she stayed with them until darkness was thick as a wall and the small circle of fire barely broke it. She could hear whatever lived in the canal moving through the brambles. She was unprepared for it, for all of it. She felt the cold tapping of fear again, drawn tight across her temples, over her chest. She pressed her fists into her ears until it retreated. Across the fire one of the fishermen studied her.

Do you know, he said when he caught her eye, about the canal thief? It lives in the water and walks on the land.

The other men laughed or hissed between their teeth. They had their rods by their sides like weapons. She could see the grease from the meat on their hands and faces. Their long limbs were cut off by darkness like amputees. One of them gestured to the bags beside him. She could see fish scales, a round button eye.

Things go missing in the night, he said and shrugged. They laughed again, and she thought that they must be making up stories to try and scare her.

As she walked away she heard them following her, and she crouched in the bushes and waited until they had trudged past and then, giving up, gone back the way they'd come, towards their fire. She did not know what they would do if they found her, only that it would be nothing good. She thought that if anything went missing in the night they must have been the ones to take it; their heavy pockets, what they buried beneath the bodies of the fish in the plastic bags. She heard their voices for a long time, and then they were cut off and there was only the sound of the water and the bushes; the scream of a fox or a hunting owl. In the dark she could not fit the tent poles into the right places and she gave up and lay in her sleeping bag again and tried to sleep but could not.

The Hunt

In the morning the dog had thrown up in the corner of the room and was sitting watching me from the door as if he knew that was the last straw. Perhaps he hated Travelodges as much as I did. I had never been able to conceive of people who liked staying in hotels or hostels, camping in fields. I did not dream of Italy or Peru or New Zealand. I dreamed of a room in which I knew where all the exits were and had nailed the curtains to the wall. That is the last straw, I said, and he seemed, almost, to smile.

I sat in McDonald's and searched for you on my laptop. Every time a child walked past they gave the dog half their burger, most of their ice cream. He wasn't, I thought, on a diet any more. I felt a sense of benevolence towards him. I answered a couple of emails. I was supposed to be finishing work on *break*. I was supposed to be back already. I had not taken a holiday or sick day for four years. They could wait. I had a sudden flash that maybe I wouldn't go back, wouldn't even tell them, wouldn't ever turn up again. I was the same as you: less a person and more a hole cut away from everything.

On the publishing house website there was a photo of me: flash-stunned, toothpaste on the collar of my jumper, a gap between my front teeth. My email address was there too, along with an office phone number. If you had ever wanted to find me you could have. It would not have been difficult for you. But there was nothing of you anywhere on the Internet. It was not the first time I had tried, but I checked and checked again. The dog sat on his bony haunches and caught chips a kid threw to him across the room. I pretended he was not my dog. I looked for you everywhere I could think. It was like trawling the water for bodies, needles in haystacks, a wild-goose chase; my favourite was: a bootless errand. There was no sign of you, there was no dust left behind by you, you were without footprints. It was frustrating all over again.

I didn't notice how long I'd been there until the lights around the forecourt of the service station started coming on. The cars swizzled their headlights, reversed out of spaces. There was something about service stations that made them similar to the way the river had been. No one lived there because their lives were going well. I only realised that after we'd left.

There was, finally, something. Maybe. The light on the screen was bright enough to hurt my eyes. I pushed the laptop closed. If I made the decision to leave right then I could be back at my desk the next day. I would not ring the morgues or hospitals. In a year I would have forgotten everything that had started to come back to me over the last few days; in ten I would not be able to bring your face to mind. By the time I was old I would have invented a whole new childhood, a tidy-haired mother who died young but quietly. Whatever it was I could feel moving towards me would recede until it was gone. Nothing would go missing in the night. In my head you said, *Stop shouting, Gretel, it's just a dream.* I was so nervous. Nervous in a way I could not remember feeling for a long time. I opened my laptop again. It was not you. It was not Marcus either – there was as little of him online as there was of you – but it was a couple who shared his last name and lived in a town not far away. I ate crisps by the handful so I wouldn't start to panic. The dog sat and looked up at me with his mouth open.

You'll be sick, I said, and then almost choked on a sharp one. Perhaps, I thought, Marcus knew where you were. Perhaps – I jammed a handful of crisps in and the dog grumbled, rolled on his back – you were with him. Perhaps that was where you went, where you had been all along.

There were records of his parents on some different sites. Enough to create a trail. The woman came up on a school website. A teacher. Involved in the forest school; recently organised a trip to the National Gallery, to a farm. She did not look like Marcus. I was disappointed. There was a restaurant review on TripAdvisor where she gave her full name and email address as if it was a CV. *We came here on Thursday as a last-minute decision. I had the chicken. My husband had the bolognese. The children also had bolognese. We would come here again. I had some wine, which was fine. My husband was not impressed with the waiter.* Besides the mention of him on TripAdvisor there was less of the man. I couldn't find a photo or any record of a job. He had left a review, though, on a car mechanics' website. Three stars and his full name.

They could, of course, be anyone. I said it out loud to myself. I went to the car and got the map out of the glove compartment, laid it out on the table in the McDonald's. I remembered how you used to say that we were nowhere, that we were outside everything. As if the place we were moored wasn't on the maps; geography didn't apply to it. I ate a second bag of crisps, fed the dog four of them. They could be anyone but – I leaned over the map – they lived near enough to the spot we'd been on the river to possibly be Marcus's parents. It wasn't a mapless place after all.

The River

What went missing in the night: the mud from the edges of the riverbanks, the rabbits in their cavernous burrows, the moorhens that slept on the low branches, stray dogs wandering where they shouldn't, the rows of fish from the fishermen's camp, silver hooks, the neighbourhood cats and everything they had – in their turn – hunted and eaten: mice, blind fumbling moles, broken-winged birds.

The next day Margot watched the land quickly become wilder. The canal fell away to a river called the Isis. It was very cold. Her hands were cut from brambles and red with small bumps from the nettles. She ran out of bread, wished she'd eaten it more sparingly. Her dreams before she'd left had been neat as bus timetables, filled with doors and square walls, things cut exactly in half, bowls of fruit. The dream she remembered from the night before was stuffed with dirt, tangled with roots, dank with water. She could feel the things Fiona had said just before she'd told her to go, filled the bag for her.

It took her a while before she realised someone was following her. The river had a habit of taking sound and swinging it around. Now and then she thought she could hear her mother calling through the undergrowth. Her footsteps seemed louder than they should. When the sun was high in the sky she stopped to rest. On the path behind her the sound of her footsteps continued for a moment after she stopped walking.

She relieved herself into a hole in the dirt. Down the path there was the sound of a bird taking off, shrieking, across the water. Someone cleared their throat but when she looked there was no one there. She thought about the canal thief who lived in the water and walked on the land. She wondered what it would look like. She thought that it must have webbed hands and feet for swimming and thin fingers for stealing. She thought about the fishermen and the way they had looked at her across the lowering fire, their open hands and how they had laughed.

She walked on. The footsteps did not belong to her. They were steadier and heavier than hers and they fell silent a beat later than hers stopped and began a moment after hers started. The path is straight, she thought, they are only walking in the same direction. Except she did not believe that. She had seen nothing but herons and half-sunk barges all day.

She walked until the sky started dipping into the water. The fearful thoughts were as long as the thorns on a blackberry bush. She wished she'd learned more before she left: how not to be so afraid, how to make a campfire, how to speak to strangers. She wished she had learned what to do when someone was following. To the side the foliage loosened, opened out. She turned and went down the bank, slipping and nearly falling, fists clenched at her side. She dropped, lay flat on her belly. Looked over the slope and up towards the towpath.

It was one of the fishermen. She did not recognise his face only knew the colour of his waterproof. He carried a metal box which rattled. He paused on the path, seemed to be studying her footprints in the dirt. She was afraid of his body. He took up more space than she thought he was owed. She put her head down into the wet leaves and held her breath. He had followed her a long way. The other fishermen – she was certain – were waiting for him to find her. He was like the canal thief: he took what he wanted, he lived in the water but had come out to follow her on the land.

For comfort she went over everything in the house that she'd loved: the round buttons on the dishwasher and washing machine, the straight edges of the shoe horn and the apples from the tree when they were too hard to eat and fell in strong winds. Something moved across the ground. She imagined that the man's eyes were like two green marbles and his hands the tapering ends of tongs. There was a noise, closer now. She raised her head up off her hands. The man was gone, but there was something else. The last of the day was coming through the bank of trees and made a shadow out of the trunks and the slight slope and the animal. She could smell the resin from the bark. The ground itched with woodlice, millipedes, a moth crawled along her arm. The animal was longer than a human on all fours. She closed her eyes and thought about the symmetry of traffic lights, the cores of fruit, the hands of clocks. When she looked again whatever had been there before had vanished. Margot lay there for a long time and felt the cold tighten around her joints, into her fingers. Her mind tried tricks of logic. She thought: it was a badger, it was a fox, it was only the shadow of a tree. But she knew the creature she'd seen had been none of these. It was the canal thief.

At some point she got up, lifted her rucksack, walked away. It was afternoon and the day felt different, impossible. Every tree was the man or the creature that had come after. She lowered her head into the hook of her hood, trudged on. Dozed while walking so that the river spiralled up like a skewer, hung over her head, seemed about to fall.

There was the slow return of industry: empty gas holders sunk into their metal frames, concrete chimneys. The grubby outskirts of a city or town: small terraced houses with train tracks running past their windows, the water dirty and low in the ground, the boats jammed nose to tail, the thin, stripped trees.

She had been walking for hours and her bad leg had stopped obeying orders, dropped her near the hedge. There was smoke from some of the boats. The freeze that was coming had hardened the trees. She could hear them clacking against one another.

Red sky at night, the man on the boat moored nearest her said, shepherds' delight. I can smell it.

She pulled her legs up to her chest. He was standing at the aft end of the boat, not watching her but busy with something in his hands. Beneath the rim of his hat she could see the shadowed cliff of his sharp nose, the sag beneath his eyes. The water was dark under the hull of the boat. She tried not to look at it, not to think about what the fishermen had said about the canal thief; tried not to think about what she'd seen in between the trees.

It's not warm, he said. He was working at the thing in his hands. I've got lamb stew and some bread that I made earlier. I can make tea if you'd drink it.

She knew better. Began gathering the bags together, pinching at her legs to bring them back. He had put down what he was doing. He had his head tipped to one side, as if listening to something she could not hear. She heaved herself up, started away.

He said, That's not necessary. Ducked his bony shoulders down and into the barge.

She stood waiting, unsure. One of the factories behind her shoulder was making a great whooping sound. She could smell the burnt sugar. Standing, the hunger was clearer, a weighty hole in her belly. The paint on the man's boat was so peeled she couldn't tell its colour: beat up, rust along the lintel and in strips down to the water. There was enough light yet to see a couple of hanging pots at one end but nothing plantlike inside them. He came back out. She should have gone and knew it. Started on, faster, dragging her leg, afraid now that he would follow her the way the fishermen had done.

It's OK. I'll put it down, he said. And I'll step back. I'll step back until I'm on the boat again.

She stopped. He came awkwardly off the side of the boat, moved a few feet forward and then bent, left the bowl in the space between them, retreated. The steam rose. She went forward, watching him, and picked up the bowl, returned to the bush. The first mouthful blistered her throat, her tongue. She shoved in some bread to ease it. The stew was good and hot, the lamb was in great chunks, crystalled with fat. The bread had a brown crust thick as her thumb and pale, spongy insides. She ate it all and when she was done raised the bowl to her face and licked it till she could see the ceramic underneath. He'd brought out a cup of tea when she wasn't looking, put it down a few paces from her. She picked it up, sat holding it tightly in her hands until it felt as if it might burn her fingerprints off.

That too weak?

She shook her head.

What? he said.

No.

All I do is eat. He wrapped the fingers of one hand around the wrist of the other. It was narrow as an iron pipe. When I'm not fishing I spend all day cooking and then all evening eating. I eat enough for five men. Five or six. Sometimes it feels as if there are six men inside me, like birds, open-mouthed. I eat and eat to feed them but I stay looking like this. You understand? He picked up the object he had been busy at before, held it to show her. It's a decoy, he said. I've been working on it a while. You know what that is?

No.

He rubbed his hands over it, turning it between his fingers. It's like a lure, a popper. Put it on the end of a rod and catch fish with it. I've had this in mind for a bit. It's big, you see. He weighed it in his bony hands. It's made to catch something bigger. I'm carving it. He picked up the knife to show her.

She was no longer afraid of him. He seemed to have more words than he could keep inside him, no one to give them to.

More? He mimed drinking.

Yes, she said and pushed up from the ground, put the cup between them. He walked oddly, almost a sidle, pushing one foot forward first as if testing for loose ground. She wondered if he was mimicking her. It had happened before. His foot tapped into the cup, almost knocking it over. As he moved back towards the boat with the cup she heard the sound of his breath rattling in the back of his throat. The water had lost its colour.

The sky was going the same way. It was getting colder, like a dial had been turned.

I made it stronger this time, he said, putting the cup down between them. I don't know your preference. It won't put hairs on your chest. I gave that up. I don't know your preference. My name's Charlie. What's yours?

She hesitated. She did not want to tell him her name and was not sure why. Marcus, she said. He seemed not to hear her. He had a book under his arm that he got out, held up for her to see. It had got so dim she could not make out the title.

I'm no good at them. Even if I could read it, he said.

What is it?

Questions. Tricks. When I was your age I could answer like this. He raised a hand, clicked two fingers. Boys are good at things like this: logic, working it out. I never had a boy but if I did he would be good at solving puzzles.

He moved back onto the edge of the boat, the book clutched to his side, other hand scouting for purchase. He was, she realised, blind. He sat down awkwardly, moving his long legs.

Are you good at these?

I don't know, she said.

I've memorised a couple. Try this one. In a forest not far from Poitiers there is a barn. It is empty except for a man who is hanging, dead, from the ceiling. The rope around his neck is ten feet long and his feet are three feet off the ground. The nearest wall is twenty feet away from the man. It is not possible to climb up the walls or along the rafters. The man hanged himself. How did he do it?

I don't know.

He shook his head, I don't know either. He kicked a foot against the edge of the boat. You see. They're tricky.

Maybe. Do you remember another one?

It was as hard as the first. She did not know the answer. Neither did he. He took up the lure again and began to whittle at it. He was bone and rafters but his hands looked strong and moved well over the wood. A little later he brought out some blankets and left them on the ground.

I don't remember any more, he said. Maybe you could read one?

He left the book between them. There was a square of light from the boat. She moved into it, taking the blankets with her, opened the book and read slowly from it.

There are two sisters: one gives birth to the other and she, in turn, gives birth to the first. Who are the two sisters?

She put her head down onto the triangle of her arms. The blankets smelled of old smoke and onions. She thought maybe she knew the answer though it wouldn't stick. Slid and rattled around in her.

The Hunt

The mechanic looked weighted wrong, the way someone just returned from space must do, scrawny-legged. I thought he might refuse to give me the address but he didn't seem to mind, wrote it down on the back of a scrap of newspaper. Even going to the stable where we'd lived didn't feel the same, as if I was as close to finding you as I'd ever been.

The dog and I circled around the block a couple of times, building courage. The houses all looked the same. The dog sighted a squirrel, set off. I was walking fast after him when I saw the right house number. No going back. The man who opened the door had his arms full of toys, glasses askew, hair receding in triangles from his forehead. He was sweating and gestured me in and I followed without having to explain why I was there. Maybe I had the sort of face people don't look twice at. The dog came barrelling in after me and we were rushed by children. I waited for the dog to bite one of them and for us both to be asked to leave. Gruffalo! one of them shouted. The man took me into the kitchen and closed the door. He offered coffee and then made me tea, barely brewed, mostly milk. He did not look like Marcus. The veins on his cheeks were broken, his nose sat square against his face. He let out a huff of air.

So the washing machine's been broken for nearly a week now, I think maybe it's the pipe, he said and then looked at me properly for the first time. There was snot on the front of my linen dress and something stuck to my shoe. You're not here for the washing machine.

No, I said. Sorry.

Don't be sorry. They didn't come yesterday either. Did I offer you coffee?

I held up my mug and started talking before I could stop myself:

I knew your son. I met him on the canal but I haven't seen him for a long time. I wondered if he came back here. I'm looking for my mother and I think he might know where she is.

He was shaking his head before I'd finished. There was a slight tremor in his hands, like the warning before a quake. You've made a mistake. He swung the door of the kitchen open, gestured out into the sitting room. The children were bum cheek to bum cheek on the floor, the sickly glow of the screen on their upturned faces. All but the last one, who was rolling across the carpet with the dog in sniffing tow, nappy coming loose. The man pointed to him. His name's Arthur, after my grandfather. The rest are all girls.

You don't have any more children? Any older children? He had a limp. I caught myself miming it and stopped. I had been certain. Never mind. I whistled for the dog but he didn't seem to notice. Don't worry, I said. You're right. I must have made a mistake. I'll leave you to it.

I was almost at the door. There was a Russian word which meant to jump one after another. *Povskakat.* Even now I was jumping after you, mindlessly. I was at the door, twisting the handle, calling for the dog whose name I did not know. Dog, I called.

A limp? the man said.

I turned back. The children had gathered, hands clasped in front of them.

Yes, I said. His left leg. It dragged.

The man's name was Roger and I knew he wanted me to stay until his wife – whose name he said was Laura – got back, by the way he kept the children ferrying things to me: glasses of water, pieces of buttered toast. I watched him as he moved, gathering up handfuls of washing, a dirty nappy, fallen toys. I tried to see the imprint of Marcus on him. Do you remember the way he looked? Taller than you with hunched shoulders, that dark bowl haircut and anxious eyes. You used to say that I had the same eyes as him, a bit heavy around the lids, lined before our time. One of the children spoke loudly at my elbow.

What?

What's your dog called? said the girl. She had her hair in four or five bunches that stuck out from the top of her head. There was a picture of a confused-looking sheep on her dress.

He doesn't have a name, I said and tried to think desperately what a person might do to make conversation with a small child. What do you want to call him?

She looked undone by the responsibility, couldn't answer. The others proffered options, shouting over one another. Roger was at the window, looking out at the street. The hair at the nape of his neck was a little long. I had never been good with children and they always seemed to know it, pay me close attention. They had made what they described as a shortlist of possible dog names which was very long and mostly comprised of animals: Dodo, Kitty, Pig. I tried to shake them off, moving around the room. There were toys in all the places alcohol would normally be. There were child locks on all of the cupboards but nothing to hide. One of the children took my hand and held on with an iron grip while I subtly tried to shake her loose. Otter, she said, what about Otter?

Do you need the bathroom? I asked her. She didn't answer but we went up the stairs all the same, hand in hand. When I reached the top I had the sudden worrying thought that I'd misunderstood, got things all wrong. How many children must go missing, wander off, every year? There were signs of destruction, toys with no heads, holes in the walls, the handle to the bathroom pulled right off. The child took me into her room and picked things up, showed them to me. I went along the corridor and into the big bedroom at the end before I could stop myself. There were photos of the man and the woman who must be Laura. They were younger, colourfully clothed. I passed my hands through the hangers in their wardrobe. On the far wall there was another small photo in a green frame. I leaned in. The child in the photo had its head turned away, a hand thrust out towards the camera. Still it was clear. The slice of face, the edge of a nose and mouth, even the way he held his shoulders. It was Marcus. His hair curly and longer than it had been when we knew him.

This is Mummy and Daddy's bedroom, the child said from the doorway.

I took a breath. I know that.

We went back down the landing. She had decided – power of suggestion – she did need the bathroom and wouldn't let me go downstairs until she had gone.

You haven't been here before, she said.

I didn't remember being so logical as a child. I remembered you telling me that I was a stone-cold liar and being shocked at the idea. It had never occurred to me that what I was doing was lying. Maybe your leaving was the same. Maybe it never occurred to you that what you were doing was abandonment.

No.

Are you going to be here tomorrow?

Probably not.

You could take us to school.

I could if I were here.

My name's Violet. What's your name? Are you Margot?

I opened the cabinet above the sink. Who's Margot?

Silly, she said, swinging her dimpled knees back and forth from the seat, wriggling. Margot's Mummy's first baby. She is old and she is gone but she would have loved us. Do you love us?

I turned and looked at her. She was staring at me sternly, elbows resting on her legs. I need to wipe now.

Go on then. Have you met Margot before?

Have you? she said.

Yes, I think so.

She pulled enough paper off the roll for three large children. It struck me that maybe she hadn't learned how to do it by herself yet and I was doing her parents an unasked-for favour.

We have never met her because she is gone, she said.

Dead?

She hopped off the toilet and wrangled her twisted underwear back up. What, she said looking at me, is dead?

I pretended I hadn't heard her. Downstairs I stood next to Roger at the counter and we watched the fish fingers he'd made for the children's dinner vanish under the table where the dog was waiting.

Otter, Violet kept saying, Otter do you want a finger? Otter, Otter, Otter.

I knelt down next to the dog. How about it, Otto? I said and he looked up and then turned away as if he wasn't certain. Roger was clear-eyed and the red had withdrawn a touch from his cheeks. I watched his hands shaking and wondered if you and he would understand one another. The way two people refusing drinks at a pub understand one another.

Margot is Marcus? I said.

He didn't seem surprised that I knew. In that house information must never stay secret very long. I could see Violet keeping an eye on me as she ate her peas. She thought we had become, I realised, allies of a sort. I don't know, he said. Maybe. She had a limp. Had it from the beginning. Had it when we found her.

What do you mean *found her*?

He closed his eyes very carefully and kept them shut. There was the sound of the front door opening. The children broke like a rugby team and Otto ran with them barking. I could hear the voice of a woman asking whose dog it was. I watched Roger's face changing, loosening a little. We went into the sitting room. The woman put her bag down on the floor and looked me up and down. What's going on? The children were gathered around, balancing on the sofa arms.

She's here about Margot, he said. She knew her.

Margot, one of the children yelled and the others took up the call. The woman raised her hands in the air. Everyone, she shouted, to bed.

I was downstairs on my own for almost an hour. I took Otto out into the garden, lay in one of the deckchairs and listened to the quiet noises from the house. I'd always felt that our lives could have gone in multiple directions, that the choices you made forced them into turning out the way they did. But maybe there were no choices; maybe there were no other possible outcomes. I couldn't anyway imagine you and me somewhere like this, though maybe it had, at times, crossed your mind. A house by the railway, a garden, you waiting for me there after school. For a moment I thought I saw lights in the windows of the shed at the end of the garden but then they were gone and I decided it must only have been reflections from the house.

Laura came out and stood next to the deckchair. Looking up at her I realised that she was older than I'd originally thought, over the hill of fifty, too old for children as young as she had.

I wondered if someone would come, she said. Tell me something I didn't want to know. You know that feeling of running on a single rail?

I wanted to tell her she wouldn't believe how much I knew it but instead I said, I think so.

It was never over. That's why we told the children about her. Because we were thinking about her all the time.

She wasn't a she when I met her, I said.

She shook her head. Well, she had a limp? Dragged her leg?

Yes.

And she was a bit awkward, not quick to talk?

Yes.

She studied me. You're younger than her.

I was only a child, thirteen if I've calculated right. I lived with my mother on a boat. Marcus, Margot, was there for a month one winter.

It was her.

Maybe, I said.

There was a silence, longer than comfortable. The dog scrabbled away, hunting through the dim bushes.

You have lots of children, I said and wished I hadn't spoken.

She sat on the edge of the deckchair. She was very close, her hands folded in her lap. We tried after Margot was gone to have some of our own, but it was too late or we couldn't to begin with. We weren't any good without them. It took us a long time to realise that. So we adopted. I used to think – less so now but often – that one day Margot would come back and see how we'd replaced her.

She stood up and whistled Otto to a spot of dirt in one of the flowerbeds, kicked at it with her boot until he began to dig. She put her hands in her pockets, stood watching him. I thought about Marcus and the time spent with him on the river and she must have been thinking about him too because she said:

What happened to her?

I took a deep breath and tried to think of something better to say, something – at least – sufficient, a form of comfort. I could think of nothing. I don't know, I said.

The River

In the morning Margot and Charlie sat out on the towpath and ate flat, thick pancakes with so much chilli the batter was red and Margot's eyes watered for an hour afterwards. Mostly he talked and she listened. He told her about being younger and driving the canals, up to the Birmingham fleet of locks; across to the Severn estuary crossing, down south as far as a person could go, up north as far as a person could get. More often though he'd stayed around that part of the country, driven back and forth the old routes.

His sight had seeped away slowly. First, he said, there was a splotch of fog near the bottom corner of his right eye. For a while, a week perhaps, he'd thought it was something following him out on the water, cruising along, a smudge on the landscape that kept pace with him. Except then the same thing happened to the other eye. The fog grew, so that once he was so distracted he drove straight rather than taking a turn, ploughed into another boat. Knew then he only had so long. Fixed the lantern on to the front of the boat and drove through the dark, through every day. It was what he knew. He would do it until the last inch of vision was gone.

One morning he woke blind and could not drive again.

He wrapped his hand around his wrist, showed her how thin it was; talked once more about the lure he was making. He told her that he missed driving.

Why? she said.

Why what?

Why did you drive so much?

She thought perhaps he wouldn't answer and felt embarrassed for asking.

I was looking for someone, he said eventually. I was looking for someone for years and years. He wouldn't say more. Grumbled something beneath his breath and turned away.

You got a cold? he said when she sniffed.

Yes.

Blow it out onto the bank.

She did as she was told, leaning over the muddy path and pressing one side of her nose.

What colour is it? he said.

Green.

You've got an infection. Come onto the boat.

He went down without waiting for her to follow. She was not afraid of him any more. Something about his blindness or the sadness of what he'd said about looking and looking for someone for years without finding them. The boat was very tidy, everything in its place. There were four frying pans hung from the wall, cups of spoons and forks. It was a relief to be on the boat. The canal thief lived in the water and walked on the land, but she did not think it would come onto that boat. She did as he instructed her, boiled the kettle over the gas flame, filled a bowl and then held her head over it.

Afterwards he cooked while she sat watching. He cooked spices in oil and they were so hot the boat was filled with a heat shimmer and both of them coughing and spluttering, retreating to the deck for air. He said it was pork belly and showed her the line of fat. He called her son or lad and she understood he did not know she was a girl. Once, when she was younger, Roger – her father – had put a bowl on her head rather than taking her to the hairdresser's and cut a straight line. For weeks afterwards – catching anxious sight of herself in reflections – she'd been surprised. She looked quite like the boy who lived next door and it had taken so little to achieve it.

They sat out on the deck and drank tea that she made for them.

I'm looking for my child, he said halfway through a sentence on some other matter. She sat very still. He seemed intent on what he had said, rocking a little so that the boat rocked with him, as if he and it were tied together. I've been looking for her for ten years. Maybe it's longer. She got taken. She was small, never lied. Her mother took her away.

He emptied out the rest of his tea into the water. There were constellations in the sky. Laura – her mother – had tried to teach her their names once but she had not kept them well, retained only fragments: bear, dog, solitary. She missed her parents. She felt the missing in the bones of her wrists and ankles, on the back of her tongue. She barely heard him when he spoke.

What?

I said: where are you going?

The sky rocked back towards her. She did not want to tell him what she had been told; what she would have done if she'd stayed with her parents. Still it was impossible not to offer him something in return.

Do you believe, she said, that if you knew what was going to happen you would be able to not do it?

What do you mean by that?

The thought was cluttered in her head. She did not know how to say it out loud. She did not think she would ever do that – speak it out. Did speaking something make it exist in a way that it only partly had before?

Do you think that life is a straight line?

A line? He seemed to think about it. No. Not a line.

Could you, she said and wondered if she shouldn't, have changed it if you'd known your daughter would be taken? If someone had told you what was going to happen.

I would have, he said. I would have stopped her.

She could see his breath in the air between them. The bone in her bad leg picked up the cold and sang with it.

The way I see it, he said, life is a sort of a spinning thing. Like a planet or a moon going round a planet. Do you understand?

Yes, she said though she wasn't sure she did.

Life is like that. Sometimes it's facing one direction but only for a second and then it's spinning and spinning, revolving on its base so fast it's impossible to really see. Except sometimes you catch a glimpse and you sit there and you know that's what it would have been like if things had gone differently, that is the way it could have been.

They sat. It was not quiet but filled with river noise, the chuck of some bird she did not know a little way down, the sound of people in other moored boats. She could see the factories set against the darkening sky, the outskirts of the city.

What is it that you were going to do? he said.

She held the thought carefully in her head. The words were spiked with barbs, unsettling as hot coals. Someone said I'd do something to my parents if I didn't leave, she said.

He sat and seemed to muse on this for a moment and then spat a glob from the side of his mouth into the water.

The river followed the same route as the train and she was woken in the tent by the sound of its passing. It was harder – lying awake, the chill through the blankets – not to think about the reason she had left. She got up, unzipped the tent enough to see the almost-starred sky above her, cut through with light pollution from some nearby place, the path black as the water.

She would leave without saying anything, go back to the house on the river, the end of the garden sloping down like a lathe to the canal. What had been said was not a truth only a suggestion of one way it might go. And if she knew what was coming she was certain she could avoid it. Like a car crash.

Another train went past, close enough she felt the breath of it. The rooms of white-lit train carriages, the faces looking out.

She zipped up the tent. Pulled the blankets over her head. She had always believed that some people knew more than others and one of those people had told her what she would do. If Margot went back she would kill her father. If she went back she would ... She could not yet think of the second. It was not in a language that could fit in the hollows of her cheeks. It tasted like dust, like gone-off yogurt or burnt toast.

The Hunt

I sat at Laura and Roger's kitchen table and listened to them talk. There was static from the baby monitor, wavering in and out. There was a sense of purging, of relief. They had been waiting a long time to speak these words, to spill them onto the table, to look down at them.

When Laura was in her early twenties her ancient aunt had died and left stacked boxes of *Private Eye*, crumbling teabags, stained toilets, a house. It was damp and some of the doors were locked or swollen shut. In the hall were bowls of keys which seemed to open nothing. The garden had an apple tree whose roots were bringing down the fence, a small crumbling shed. Roger liked the tiny rooms, the narrow crawl space in the attic, the sound of the water against the white walls at the bottom of the garden. It was, Laura said, the way they'd lived then: borrowed houses, fast jobs. They were stone poor. They were, Roger said, poor as church mice.

I could see them. Long-haired, hand in hand, reading the menus in restaurant windows but never going in, walking home late, trailing street lamps. There were no children yet but at times – in the mornings, barely awake – they spoke about the names they would call them.

They had been there three months and the local charity shops were full of everything they'd tidied, boxed up, given away. The glass of their bedroom window was thin as just-made ice. There were flat-faced owls that hunted nearby, cats that fought on the arched bridge that the homeless came and slept beneath.

It could be anything, Laura mumbled when they heard a noise one night. She rolled over, slept again. Roger couldn't. The noise went on, insistent. He put on slippers, Laura's old dressing gown, a hat he found by the front door. Beside the house the path ran on to the bridge and then down on either side to the river. He stood on the road listening. It was not owls hunting or cats fighting. It was, he thought, a child.

It was so dark he couldn't see the path. Couldn't see where the water started. He followed the sound, foot over foot. He worried that he would trip, hit his head, fall into the water and never be found. He kept on. There was a dustbin on the path, half in a bush, blocking the way. The child was inside, wrapped in a blanket, sucking on strips of orange peel and weeping. Something biblical about it, Roger said, something accidentally mythic. He picked her up, tucked her against his chest, carried her back up to the house.

The girl had come to them. She stopped crying when either of them held her, ate the fish fingers they cooked by the dozen, seemed to listen when they spoke to her, wept when they left the room. In the night when she woke crying Roger went into the room and stood over the bed. She stiffened at his presence, alert. They listened together to the noise of the river on the walls of the house, the dishwasher downstairs, the mice that lived in the attic. They'd been rolling towards that moment, Roger thought, rolling without noticing down the slopes of the hills towards it.

The adoption process had been surprisingly fast. No one came forward to claim her. No one else wanted her. The woman in charge of the adoption agency visited twice a day for the first week. A large woman called Claudia with a pierced eyebrow who sat so quietly they often forgot she was there at all. It was difficult to see anything but the girl, the way her eyes followed them about the room. On her final visit Roger showed Claudia to the door. Something had been worrying him.

Why do you think no one came forward? he asked.

She was nearly at her car already. She came back slowly. Lots of reasons.

Why do you think?

She pointed down towards the water. I spent some time on the canals when I was starting out. Not an easy job. They have their own communities down there, their own rules. They don't call the police or child services when something goes wrong. They have their own authority. It's a different world. They left her on the path because they wanted someone else to find her. No one has come forward because no one is looking for her.

They went through different names for the girl every week, every day. They had not, Laura mourned, had time to prepare. They were not ready. One day Roger called her Margot and it stuck like a pin in a wall. Margot.

I worried there was something wrong with her, Laura said.

Like what? I said.

Anything could have been wrong. I couldn't sleep, she said. I couldn't help thinking about them.

What do you mean? About who?

Her parents. Her genetic parents. All their genes inside her wreaking secret havoc. People give more to their children than hair and eye colour, don't they? Children are a map of genes.

There was a blare of noise from the baby monitor and I watched them both stiffening, but after a moment there was nothing for a long time and they sat back, started speaking again.

Margot was broad-chinned, straight-nosed, flat-handed with thick eyebrows that made her look often suspicious and, sometimes, surprised. She was big for her age, knees like a horse's, knuckles too large for her fingers. She was a late crawler, an even later walker and – when she finally started – it was clear why. Her left leg hitched a little behind the other like a rusting trailer dragged by a new car. The doctor had a watch on a chain that she swung for Margot and that Margot was afraid of. The doctor pressed at the shy leg, edged it straight, held the foot in her hands. Laura stared at the X-ray, the white lines, the etchings of dark. The doctor put her pen in her mouth and pointed at the abnormality: the bone in Margot's left leg twisted away as if from strong light or pressure. When she was seven the brace was removed. In the long winters the bones in the leg burned; in the summers she thought she could feel the water gathering in her joints; in autumn and spring she remembered these feelings and would never quite walk straight again.

She was cautious, suspicious even – Laura said – as if everything they tried to teach her was a trick. She did not believe there could be words such as obtuse, ketchup, diatribe, harlequin. She did not believe that what they planted in the ground would grow. Still, she was good with her hands, enjoyed the slow, careful walks they took around the town and down on the towpath. They forgot more and more every day that they had not been the ones who created her.

Occasionally Roger would come upon her sitting on her bed, studying the ceiling where Laura had fixed glow-in-the-dark stars in uneven, incorrect constellations. What you looking at, Margot? he'd say and she would turn that band of concentration towards him, say: nothing. At times she unnerved him. She was not like the other children who Laura would sometimes pause to watch racing around the playground, throwing themselves on and off the skipping ropes, circling on their bicycles.

What did you do at school today? they would ask, and it would take her the walk home to come up with an answer, mouth pursed tight around her teeth. We drew, she said. We ran.

Where did you run?

She would frown, barely believing her own answer. We ran to the wall. We ran back again.

She was friends – as far as her parents could see – with no one except the boy next door who had thin hair and a nervous stutter. Margot would go round and they'd search together for pale, soft worms or scrabbling nests of woodlice, or they would build a dam and watch the water gather. He gave her gifts: leaves with strange vein patterns, apples with worms dug right through, coins so brown she couldn't see the queen's head.

One day he heaved himself up onto the fence between their gardens and threw a piece of paper down to her. She studied it, took it inside, gave it to Laura.

What's this?

Simon gave it to me.

Laura flattened it on the counter, read it out loud: *Will you be my girlfriend.* Laura looked at her, said nothing. Margot took the piece of paper and buried it in the garden as if she thought it would grow and grow downwards like an upside-down tree. When Simon came knocking she would not see or speak to him again. Laura watched her bury every message he sent helicoptering over the fence without reading any.

Perhaps that was the start. Those words on the page, swimming in and out of one another. She would not read, told them the words were ants which crawled, would not hold still. A young teacher spent extra time with her, spoke with enthusiasm on the progress she was making. She can read this whole book now. Except when Roger asked her to, he watched as she closed her eyes, recited from memory.

Why don't you want to read?

She clamped her mouth closed, would not speak.

Why don't you like words?

They move.

What do you mean?

They aren't for me, she said in that way she sometimes did, steely-eyed, a little frightening, like an adult lost in a child's body.

When Margot was ten Simon's family moved away and the house next door was empty for a couple of months before someone new arrived. Her name was Fiona. There was no removal van, only – one day – a woman in a red raincoat with a suitcase. They'd watched Margot's strange fascination with her, how she ran to the door at any sound from the street or sat at the upstairs windows looking for movement in the garden below. She would lie under their conjoining hedge waiting for the door to open, dirt in her hair and mouth. Pressed her ear against the walls which divided their house from the house next door. There was no sign of the woman. Margot cornered Roger and Laura at the sink or on their way out to the bins or as they came out of the bathroom. Who is she? she said. Who is she?

I don't know, they said. Why don't you go and say hello?

They gave her banana bread to take round and practised what she might say. *Hello, I live next door. My name is Margot.* She got as far as the gate and then froze, stood trembling, ran home and up to the window from where she could watch.

Roger took the banana bread himself. Fiona was painting her stairs bright yellow and had paint in her hair. She made him sausage sandwiches and sweet coffee. Insisted on reading his tarot cards and then laughed loudly at his expression when she did. He liked her. She was straight talking and laughed easily. She had hardly any furniture and – when she opened the oven to put in the sausages – had to take out the shoes she'd been keeping in there. He heard himself, and was surprised, inviting her over for dinner. He and Laura were friends with few people. At the door he told her that Margot, their daughter, liked her very much already. She looked pleased and had taken his hand.

Fiona came for dinner the next day. She was tall as a tree, stick-thin, red-mouthed. Margot did not even pick up her cutlery. Fiona ate three potatoes from the salad and then the middle of a slice of bread, drank a glass of water and went home. Margot knelt on her chair and held the intact crust of bread, looked through the hole at her parents. After that Fiona was there for dinner often. Margot was a little afraid of her. She was elemental, alchemical. Margot followed her around, watched as she washed up, ate an apple, went into the bathroom. Roger and Laura observed her intense observation of Fiona with interest and amusement. They had never seen her so intrigued by another person. She was afraid of the postman and the man who came to fix the sink; at school they were told she kept to herself, spoke rarely in class.

What do you think it is about her? Laura said one evening after Margot was asleep and they were sitting in the garden. Why do you think Margot is so fascinated? Roger tipped his head to look at the sky.

I might be wrong but do you remember the way she was with Mrs Twigg? Roger asked. Mrs Twigg had been Margot's favourite teacher in reception, an imposing woman in her late fifties with a quiet, stern voice who frightened Roger and Laura at parents' evenings but who Margot had talked and talked about until she'd retired and moved to France. Margot had been drawn to her in the way she seemed drawn to Fiona, sucked in by them both, seemingly fascinated by something Roger and Laura could not pinpoint but that Roger thought might be age.

She's drawn to older people? Laura was sceptical. They sat in silence. Laura remembered Margot bringing home drawings from school when she was young. Her drawings were different from the other children's; they were dour, sketched in browns and blacks. Still, they went on the fridge. One had been of Roger and Laura and Margot and another figure who towered over the three of them, great dangly arms and a wide, friendly mouth. When Laura asked who it was Margot had explained it was Mrs Twigg. And so, Laura thought, it wasn't so much age as authority, a sense of benevolent control.

Once – she was eleven or twelve – Laura sat her down and told Margot that Fiona used to be a man.

Sometimes, Laura said, we don't want what we've got. Eat your porridge.

The next time she saw Fiona, in her garden hacking at weeds, Margot put her mouth to the earring-heavy lobe.

Secret? Margot said.

Fiona nodded, raised her hand and pressed it loosely over her chest. Not a soul.

Margot told her what Laura had said, that Fiona was a woman in a man's body.

That's the truth, Fiona said, like a fish still alive in the belly of a heron.

It fascinated Margot. For weeks she thought about that fish, pushing through the feathers, searching for salt water. In the mornings Fiona would be sitting in her garden and Margot would hand over a cup of tea. Can you? she'd say, and Fiona would take the eyeliner from her pocket, bend down and draw a thin moustache over Margot's lip.

Roger and Laura saw Fiona often, mostly with Margot and sometimes without; went to Chinese restaurants or on walks around the town. They got on well though some weekends she wouldn't talk much or would meet them looking stray-thin and some weekends she wouldn't turn up at all. She carried the tarot pack with her, wore a leopard-print hat pulled down to the eyebrows. Often she would send them postcards – always addressed to Margot – from wherever she was. She wrote, *The weather here is bad at the moment but I know it's going to get better.*

Margot, it was clear, loved her with a fierce, unwavering love. Followed her around the house, sat quietly listening when Fiona talked, howled with laughter – in an uninhibited way she did with no one else – at her jokes. When Fiona did card tricks or told Margot she knew when it would rain or what day the eggs would go off, Margot believed her insistently. Would not listen when Roger tried to explain that no one really knew what was going to happen before it did.

Fiona does, Margot said. Fiona knows.

She believed it, Roger thought, with a certainty and strict rigour that seemed unusual for a child her age. Once she had sat peacefully across the table from him and spoke falteringly about fate. Do you know what that means, Margot? Yes, she said, it means that we have no choice. He'd been angry at Fiona about that, though when he'd spoken to her she'd defended herself, told him she wasn't feeding her lines, Margot had come up with the thought all on her own. His daughter was like someone from another age, he thought, or someone – a less kind thought – from a cult or family of religious extremists. He watched her jaw setting when he tried gently to argue with her. She was immovable. I believe, she said, in fate.

One week when Margot was thirteen they did not see Fiona at all, and when Roger went round to her house he found it empty, the door unlocked, the electricity and water switched off. The next day there was a FOR SALE sign on the worn grass out the front. A few weeks afterwards there were removal vans outside, a new family moving in. Margot watched out the window.

It was a year before Fiona came back. The houses by the bank were flooding and people were carrying everything they owned out and up the hill. The street was filled with shadows heaving armchairs or record players above their heads. Fiona did not ring the doorbell but came to the back of the house and stood looking in through the window. She was thin, and the old raincoat was ripped and dirty. Something had happened though she would not say what. Roger took Margot upstairs to make up the bed in the spare room. He wanted to say something to her, to explain or comfort, but she seemed strangely calm, tucking in the corners of the sheet. Not for the first time he wondered where she had come from, what she'd brought with her when she arrived.

In the night they listened to Fiona roaming, talking quietly to herself. They worried about her. It did not occur to them to ask her to leave though later they would wish they had. Every morning Margot would carry a cup of tea up, leave it outside the door, bring it back down again – cold and untouched – in the afternoon. It was three or four months before Fiona would drink the tea, longer than that before she sat with them at meals. Gradually she put on weight, slept through the night, began to speak to them rather than to herself.

After she came back Margot and Fiona were – more than ever – accomplices, artful dodgers, thick as thieves. Margot accepted truths from Fiona she would accept from no one else. Believed Fiona when she told her about currents, the water table, the way the land moved. Listened when Fiona explained words like extraneous and chattel. When she had a nightmare she went into Fiona's room.

Roger would often catch the two of them – just before dawn – whispering under the blankets. He worried, a little, about those early-morning conversations, remembering that determined eight-year-old sitting at the table staring at him and talking about fate, about lives without choice. But Fiona seemed mellowed somehow, calmer, quieter. She slept more and argued less, and Margot – it was clear – loved her.

They never told Fiona where Margot had come from. Never told Margot either. It would, they decided one late night out walking, have hurt Margot in a way they could not stand to do. She might have come from somewhere else, from someone else, but she belonged with them now.

The River

In the scree of trees crows gathered and then broke apart like jigsaw pieces. It was easier – while not running – for Margot to imagine a life for herself there, a whole new body she could step inside. She was his child or – no – his sister's child; her mother was dead; she was staying until she was old enough to leave. And, even then, she would visit him; she would help him. Days would be the way they were, slow, easy. He would teach her to cook and to whittle lures, to fish with them. Maybe, even, one day they would move the boat. He would teach her to drive and – when they grew tired of living beneath the shadow of the factory, the town – they would drive away. How does a person give up everything they know? They find something to replace it. He called her son or boy and she thought: maybe. Why not?

He told her about his daughter being born on the boat, how he'd caught her in his arms and held her against his face, the wet mess of her, like something washed up on a beach. A child. His first. Like he'd dreamed. And how she began to focus on him with her serious, frowning face. Her hair grew fast, the colour of dried grass; she lengthened, grew weighty. Her balled hands, the small dome of her head. How he'd woken and she was gone. Both of them. The child and her mother. They might never have existed if it weren't for what was left behind: small socks, the bundle of blankets in the drawer where she'd slept. What was left behind: all the words she'd never learned to say; all the conversations they hadn't had.

Two days turned into three. They ate pancakes or eggs for breakfast. He worked on the lure, which he told her – over and over again – was to catch something bigger. She puzzled over the books he gave her or sat watching him fish. There was a quiet serenity.

Nights were different. Nights were tangles of what-might-have-been, of awful possibility. She was still too nervous to sleep on the boat so had pitched her tent on the towpath, took it down each morning to clear the way. The path was stony beneath her back. She woke before it was light three nights in a row. The sound of snuffling beyond the tent, movement on the path or the bank. Lying so still she didn't realise she had bitten deep into her cheeks until it was quiet again; whatever had been there was gone.

I've heard it too, he said when she haltingly told him about the noises. I thought it was a badger or a fox to begin with. They get into the rubbish. But I don't know. Maybe it's not. People are saying there's something in the water that wasn't there before. He took the lure out of his pocket, held it up. I think it has human hands and a fishy mouth.

It was the canal thief, she thought. The thing that lived in the water and walked on the land. It had followed her up the river. She closed her eyes and in the light-stuck dim she saw something scaled moving through the murk at the bottom of the canals. It did not have human hands, but if it could stand it would be as tall as one and it had a clever mind and it stole what it wanted. Behind her lids she saw that the canal thief had Fiona's face.

She was woken again on the fourth night. She sat up. There was water on the inside of the tent, a sheen of it on the walls that made her arms wet when she brushed against them. Outside the tent there was a shifting, infinitesimal. She pulled the blanket close against her ears to block anything out. She did not want to know. The sides of the tent moved, shaking. Wind. Probably. Except then there was a thundering. The noise of movement on the wooden roof of the boat. She reached for whatever she could find – the bag of leftover tent pegs – pulled the zip down, went kneeing out into the mud. There was a caterwauling. The thought of Charlie on the boat, blind, on his own, gave her a bravery she had never had before. Onto the wooden deck and swinging the double door open, down the three steps, sprawling at the bottom. The bag of tent pegs spinning away across the wooden floor. There was the sound of shouting, breakage. There was a little light from the street lamps on the road but not enough to see anything clearly. She caught only flashes of movement. She could feel her mouth stretching wide, realised she was shouting too. It was there. The canal thief. Something rushed her, fleshy, fingers tangling painfully in her hair.

Get the fuck out, someone screamed. She was barrelled aside, landed heavily. There was a face lit up by the window, the arms long as pylon wires and raised high, the agog mouth and blind fleeing eyes. She raised her hands, rolled, just missed his feet, which went thundering past. She looked past him into the dark for what must be there, for what she'd heard. There was nothing. The canal thief was not there.

Get out, he shouted. Keep away. He was rebounding off the walls, flailing whenever she got close enough to hit.

It's OK, she said and he followed her voice, arms knocking her down, following her with hands outstretched, thumbs burying in her throat. She opened her mouth to tell him she wasn't who he thought she was; she wasn't the canal thief. She opened her mouth to tell him that she couldn't breathe but there wasn't breath left to say even that. She thrashed her hands down, grappled for purchase, came away with nothing. Her vision was becoming obscured, as if by dirt. Her fingers – grasping – touched something which she clutched in her hand and then brought up mindlessly, struck as hard as she could towards the place she thought he must be.

She could hear her pulse. There was hot, painful breath in her mouth and chest. Her hands were hot too, and wet. She lay still. It was quiet. There was the smell of the potatoes and onions Charlie had cooked earlier. Light through the windows picked out the bits of the boat. What had happened? She had been sleeping. She had heard a noise. The blankness that followed frightened her. There was a weight across her legs. She found the handle of a cupboard and tugged herself upright. When she put her hand back down on the floor it landed on something sharp, metal. The bag of tent pegs, burst open. She put her flattened hand against her mouth and it was warm and salty. The weight on her legs was Charlie. She pulled her legs out from under and he flopped away. His eyes were open the way they always were, the filmed white of old photographic reels. She could feel the panic rising, yeasty, unbearable. She put her hands on his face, his bare wrists. He was cooling already. She pressed her fists into his thin chest. He did not respond. Her arms were too heavy for her body. She pressed her mouth once down on his, tried to force in the unwieldy air the way she'd seen done on television. The bursting of blood from his nose made her think he was alive still. Hands on his chest again, pressing down and down. She did not understand. There were the sounds of cars crossing nearby roads, the alarm up at the factory, voices from other boats. She tried not to look at him but small glances got in: the purpling colour of his skin, the sock on one foot pressed nearly all the way off the heel.

Eventually she made herself get up, closed the curtains, locked the door, went through the cupboards and ate a tin of beans that she found there. She took a blanket from the bedroom and put it over the body. She was wrong that it would make it easier. It only made it easier to think that he was still alive.

At some point she must have slept because it was dimmer without her noticing the change. The boat was moving gently against the bank as if another craft had just passed by. Charlie was beneath the blanket. He was – she realised properly for the first time – dead. When she stood she saw the end of the tent peg on the floor beside him and remembered clearly what had happened: her hands reaching out to both sides, the feel of the metal, the way she had brought it up and against his head. She brought her hands up hard into the sides of her face. Again time went past without her noticing. When she looked up it was so quiet outside they could have floated away, been carried right out of the city. She got up and opened the doors and stepped outside, pulling them tight behind her. There was the smell of burning rubber and the lamps a couple of streets over were extinguished, the path and water merged into black. She stood waiting for someone to come walking towards her but there was no sound or movement.

There was preservation. Later she would remember and be surprised at herself for it. On the path she bent and felt blindly for rocks, carried them in the folds of her jumper. Back on the boat she inched around the body – trying not to touch skin – pushed the rocks into the pockets of the yellowed dressing gown he was wearing. He was heavier than he looked and she wished she'd put the stones in afterwards. It was too late. She heaved with her hands beneath his armpits, the gaping sockets, the smell of his hair on her face. Got him up onto the first step and then faltered. His skin beneath her hands was doughy. She knocked the door open and levered him out onto the small deck, stood huffing in the cold. Lugged him up onto the side, held on for a moment, let him fall forward.

Three

The Weather Here Is Bad

The Cottage

You tell me you are going mad with boredom, that I cannot keep you locked up like this, that you need to get out the house.

I put the kettle on, point to the door. You aren't locked up, off you go.

That's not what I mean. Let's go somewhere. Mother-and-daughter outing. A little trip.

I cannot tell if you are joking or not but then you stand up and I see that you've found and packed an old handbag I bought years ago and never used. You're wearing a skirt, the material stretched tight across your hips and backside. I haven't been to the office for nearly a month; not since the day before I visited the morgue and, afterwards, began searching for you. It's time I went back. Take-your-deranged-mother-to-work day.

OK, I say, and you brighten.

Where are we going? you ask once and then a second time on the bus. You take the window seat, point at passing people or parked cars. Being out of the house seems to have a worsening effect and your sentences are peppered with mistakes or misunderstandings which I, quietly, correct. I am becoming your mouth. The journey is nearly an hour, and you chat away, now holding my hand, now knocking me aside with a hiss. There is a degree of innovation to the way you speak, a constant attempt at hiding or brushing over flaws. You have brought with you, tucked into the handbag, one of the notebooks we have both taken to writing in, and I watch as you attempt, now and then, to draw an image of a word that is troubling you. You do not want my help. You tut at me if I attempt to fill a pause or interpret a drawing. Be quiet, you say, be quiet. We are not friends, you are my mother. I am not allowed to pity you.

We get off the bus and walk to the office. It is the summer holidays and the streets are clogged with bodies. You dart away from me into cheese or book shops. You point and whisper comedic observations about everyone we pass. Look at his hat, what a hat that is. Is that a skirt or a belt do you think? We are, for the moment, co-conspirators the way we had been on the river. Your attention is the same as the ray from a lighthouse. I am struck dumb beneath it. I think of what it must have been like to come upon us the way Marcus did. We were kings of that place. We did whatever we wanted. You were a small deity, a quiet god. No wonder we were able to bring about what we did. No wonder we saw the Bonak in the night.

I think of the days Marcus slept on our boat, bundled up under the blankets, so close I could feel his hot breath on my face, his eyes rolling beneath the lids. You slept like the dead, but he had nightmares that sent him floundering across the mattress, knocking against the walls, talking nonsense that I would lie awake and listen to. He slept there enough nights – I think – that we came across a sort of morning routine. You on the steps out of the boat with a cigarette and a cup of coffee – a whore's breakfast, you called it. He coming slowly out of whatever nightmare he'd had like a sailor out of a storm. What do you dream? I'd ask but he could never remember. You would stub your cigarette out, stretch your white arms above your head. I'd watch his eyes turning towards you.

The office is imposing from the outside, white stone, a tall gate, wide windows. You stop on the cobbles and point.

You work here?

Yes, I say and am momentarily proud until I catch your smirk and understand you are mocking me.

We come to my floor. I worry that you will shout, make a fuss, run.

You have to be quiet, I say.

You look at me, draw a line across your mouth with your fingers. We go into the office and towards my desk. It is as I left it, the yellow citations laid out, the pens in their holder, the in tray overflowing. I do not have any photos or postcards. You open the drawers and peer inside. I see your lips moving but no words come out. Over the tops of the cubicles I see Jennifer, my boss, waving to me. When we reach her she widens her arms as if we might embrace but nothing comes of it. Lexicographers rarely hug.

Who's this then? she asks, stretching a hand out to you. I have an awful moment of wondering if I should lie. This is my friend, this is my batty aunt, this is a woman I'm looking after. Anything but the intimacy of that word. Except you have ploughed in, looping your arm through mine, tugging me so close our shoes knock together, reaching out with the other to shake Jennifer's hand.

I'm her mother. I'm Sarah.

I tell Jennifer that I'm sorry I've been away so long.

Take as much time as you need.

The understanding pity of others is a hole. I thank her, ask how everything has been going. By the time I look around you have gone. I trek back through the office. The carpet is worn by diligent feet. Some of the panels in the ceiling are out of place the way they were in my dream. I do not shout for you. I look around corners and under the tables, in the bathroom. You are nowhere. I go up and down. I have lost you again. Was this why you wanted to come out? You melt away so easily. I can feel, already, a heavy mourning in my belly. You had told me so little, explained so little. I will never understand what happened. I realise – a sharp pain – that I would miss you if you went, that it would be harder this time around.

I hear you before I see you. You are weeping, exhausted, knocked forward over my desk. An intern is hovering nearby, hands clenching and unclenching in the air. I wave him away.

What's wrong? I say.

I am furious with you. I grab you around the top of your arm and try to heave you up but you cling on, kicking. You grab the citations and crumble them. Heads are beginning to appear above the cubicles, chairs pushed back. I see between your closing fingers a couple of phrases from the word I was working on before I left. *Sustain an injury / become inoperative / amniotic fluid.* You tear them and – as I move forward again – push them into your mouth, swallow, cough out strips of yellow paper. The intern has his mouth open like a fish. I can see Jennifer moving in slow motion towards us, starting to run. You press the last piece into your mouth and seem, suddenly, calm. There are tears streaked through the city dust on your cheeks. I watch as you pocket the hole puncher on my desk and then turn back, hold out a hand which I take, not knowing what else to do.

It's fine, I say to the intern and Jennifer and the rest. Everything's completely fine.

We go back towards the stairs and down. I am shaking but you are serene, nearly radiant, wiping spit from the corner of your mouth, patting me on the shoulder.

What were you doing? I ask you. What were you doing?

I didn't remember that word. But I do now.

I pause, and you move ahead of me, purposeful, arms pumping. There is something childlike about your logic, your hands pressing the written word between your teeth, your tongue reaching out to reclaim it. The same as us on the river: eating the heart of an animal to steal its strength.

I remember, out of nowhere, being accosted at a train station by a man in a bright purple T-shirt with a piece of paper where he wanted me to write my details. He had dropped a large orange into my open hand and told me that was how much brain a person lost when they had Alzheimer's. I thought about that. The size of an orange cored right out of you.

We are both, suddenly, famished. We spin around the supermarket, filling a trolley indiscriminately. I watch you heave a whole chicken in and I say nothing. Your language decays without any attempt at reforming it. You jam sentences together, point at bread and call it eggs, seem intoxicated, electric bursts of sound escaping from you. You speak of yourself in the third person and seem to have lost the letter M entirely.

You frightened me, I tell you in the frozen aisle. You embarrassed me back there.

You look at me steadily. Your arms are filled with frozen sausage rolls and ice cream. Your eyes are the colour of mine, that unforgiving, take-no-prisoners grey.

But I love you, you say.

I do not know what to reply to that.

The Hunt

September. Roger's birthday. It was 1997. Margot was sixteen and had at the start of the year watched the sun move bodily over the moon, obscuring it.

Fiona had put on an apron and cooked lamb stew with bananas and chocolate; swore and stomped around the kitchen banging pans, sweating through the armpits of her silk dress; gave up, ordered a takeaway.

Margot decorated, moving stoically, draping the curtain rails with Fiona's pearls, lighting candles along the mantelpiece. She had half a glass of wine. Roger remembered the colour in her face, the conkers she had gathered and painted for him, wrapped up, left where he would find them. He would remember the way she looked for ever, as if she had lost the capacity for ageing and only stayed the way she was that night: the cap of hair against her face, the straight brand of her nose, her thick eyebrows creased in concentration.

Laura mostly remembered Fiona that night: quieter than normal, going back and forth from the bathroom, changing her outfit a couple of times, standing at the window and looking thoughtfully out at the bottom of the garden. Once, even, she'd gone out the back door, down to the end and stood in front of the small green shed. Laura remembered her with the hindsight of knowing what she would do; remembered her taking the last glug of wine from the bottle without offering it around, stumbling a little as she picked up the plates and took them to the sink. She had ordered Chinese for them all and been disappointed with the spring rolls. They're not crisp, she said and then said it again. They're not right.

Never mind, Roger had laughed, a little drunk. Never mind the spring rolls.

And for a moment she had given him such a look, her jaw jutting, that Roger had sat back, surprised, and the rest of them fallen quiet. Right, she'd said, shaking both of her arms and grinning toothily, never mind the spring rolls. You're right, old man. Quite right.

On Sunday their hangovers kept them in bed. Laura had got up late and made tea in the kitchen. Taken four cups up on a tray, left Fiona's in the hall outside her room, gone in to see Margot. The bed was made, and when she went looking, Laura found things missing: a jumper, Margot's walking boots. The panic did not set in then although it was close. She was gone. Not – as Laura had often seen in long, twisty nightmares – taken, but gone. Of her own volition.

When they went over and over that evening they could not help but wonder what would have happened if they had done it differently. If they'd not drunk so much; if the next day had been one of the ones Laura worked at the school and so was up early, waiting for the kettle in the chilly kitchen; if Roger had gone down to check the doors were locked the way he normally did.

*

Forgiveness, Laura said, was not something she could give. Forgiveness didn't come until a person was so tired they couldn't do anything else.

Roger had walked around the town, searching; come back with his fingers blue from the cold, his mouth a purple smear. Laura went through Margot's room looking for some kind of sign, a message or secret code which meant she had not wanted to go, she would be back soon. Fiona sat at the table drinking coffee without milk. She had her boots and coat on but she had not got up to help or spoken to the police on the phone. She was still wearing the lipstick from the night before.

Did you see her? Roger asked her. Did you hear her leaving?

I knew something, Fiona said after a moment. I knew something. It was, she said, the same as rising too fast and becoming dizzy.

She had known something and she had told Margot.

What? Laura said, what did you tell her?

Fiona closed her eyes. She was, Roger saw, crying, and he was so frightened he could barely speak. I told her she had to leave, Fiona said. I told her to go.

They posted photos on lamp posts, the windows of shops, the windscreens of cars. Went on the local news. Roger walked and walked, looking for something that no one but he would be able to see. Laura drove the roads, pulling into service stations, showing Margot's photo around, waiting to see a figure out by the rushing cars, thumbing a lift. When she got home she went into Fiona's room and searched it. She was tidy: the bed made, a small shelf of books on one wall, neat rows of toiletries. Laura pushed her hands beneath the mattress, upended it, knocked the books onto the floor and shook them out, went through the clothes in the wardrobe. They had spent all morning trying to force Fiona to tell them what she had told Margot but she'd refused and now there was nothing there in her bedroom either. There was nothing there that meant anything. Laura put everything into bags, left them out by the kerb. In the morning Fiona was gone.

They went to group meetings for people whose children had chosen to leave them. A few times Roger went to meetings for people whose children had died, but it was not the same and he'd known it. He was a fraud there. His child had not wanted to stay with them. His child had never really even belonged to them.

Laura worked instead of thinking: ran after-school clubs, got a PGCE so she could teach full time, went to cafes after work and sat in the windows marking.

Roger drank. Mostly, to begin with, he drank beer. He did not drink in pubs or when other people were around; he drank in the bathroom or took cans out in the pockets of his coat when he went walking. Later he worked his way through everything a person could work their way through. The days were not days but blanks in between sleeping. He remembered the way when she was younger Margot had spoken with such certainty about a lack of choice, a determinism. And he'd imagined – this perhaps the worst thing – her going thinking she had no choice, that all along she had been bound to leave them. He could not stand that. He would rather drink his days empty of thought than spend a moment thinking like that.

Fiona had come back eventually. The intervening years had been long, initially fraught with Roger's drinking and with trying to have children that would not come. There had been a miscarriage and a car accident in which Roger was drunk. There had been six months when Laura had lived somewhere else. There had been, also, peace, a slow return of just enough happiness they knew not to give up on one another. By the time Fiona turned up again, perhaps seven years later, they had adopted two of the four children they would later have. Roger had gone through unstable periods of sobriety but he was drinking again. In the evenings or the very early mornings he would bury the cans or bottles in the flower beds, sober up with his face in the cold grass. He'd seen things before while drinking – watched Margot clamber out of the disturbed ground, heard voices he knew weren't there. That night he'd seen lights through the window of the shed, looked for a weapon, had only the bottle he was drinking from, hefted it up, jerked the door open. They had never used the shed much and it had been, for years, filled with broken garden chairs, an old lawnmower and boxes of Christmas decorations. All of this had been tidied into piles and one of the deckchairs from the garden had been dragged in there, covered with a blanket. In the middle of the shed Fiona was crouched. He held onto the doorframe and moved the bottle higher. Fiona had looked – he said – worse than any of the times before. At moments she would catch his eye but mostly she looked over his shoulder or up at the ceiling. She was too thin, and when she ran a distracted hand through her hair it came out in clumps. There had been a moment – he admitted it – when he'd considered swinging the bottle down. Except then she would never tell them where Margot had gone.

He kept her secret for nearly a month, sneaked out dry toast and bowls of pasta, watched her swallowing the food without breathing. She hadn't spoken at all for a while, only watched him, eaten what he gave her, slept on the deckchair. Occasionally he questioned her, demanded, shouted. Occasionally he begged. She gave nothing away. He thought often about those postcards she used to write them when she went away. *The weather here is bad.* The whisper of them landing on the mat, the way he'd read them when he drank the first coffee of the day. When he eventually told Laura he thought she would throw them both out, change the locks. Except they both understood that there was only one person who might know where Margot had gone and that person was living in the shed at the bottom of their garden.

The River

Low stone bridges over the water, houses tucked together, crumbling banks. Margot ducked into the shade of a bush and watched a gaggle of overweight police officers standing on the path talking to walkers. There were mud splatters on the ironed creases of their trousers. She imagined them gathered around the boat, pressing their pale faces to the windows. She waited for them to come along the path towards her, lift her beneath the arms, tell her that they'd found a body and knew she was to blame. She had taken the book of riddles from the boat and they would find it in her bag and then there would be no doubt. She untied and retied the laces on her left shoe. One of the officers kicked some pebbles into the river and watched them sink. She closed her eyes. She thought of the way Charlie had called her boy or son, the certainty with which he'd decided she wasn't a girl. She thought about the people on the other boats, who must have seen her going down the steps or sitting with Charlie on the roof. She thought about how they would pull the body – heavy with water and weed – out of the river, the cords they would attach around him, the pulleys. When she opened her eyes the police had moved off the towpath and into cars on the road; the walkers were gone. She stood up and went on.

A memory. When Fiona had lived in the house next door Margot would go to her for breakfast and – after they'd eaten banana and peanut butter on toast – would watch her shaving. The razor moving slickly across the skin, the rasp and the hair darkening the sink, Fiona's face looking at her from the mirror. Darker and darker each time, she would say. Thicker and thicker.

She came to a boatyard with old tugs pulled out of the water for painting and rental barges stored for the winter. There was a small waterside shop that she stood outside. She was so hungry. She went into the shop. It sold great barrels of boat oil, dirty potatoes in sacks, folded paper maps of the river.

On the noticeboard she saw a poster of a missing cat, went closer to look. There were seven or eight similar posters pinned up around it, mostly for dogs and cats that had gone missing from the boats or the flats that overlooked them, but also one, she saw, for a goat that had been living in a field nearby. She took a basket and shopped sparingly, putting back half of what she first picked up.

As well as some bread and jam and bottled water, she bought a roll of cling film and a packet of razors, a pair of scissors. On the way out of the shop she looked again at the posters for the missing animals. Where were they? They had gone, she thought, missing in the night the way she had, the way Charlie had. On the path she ate four slices of bread in ravenous panic and kept walking.

*

When she slept that night the man she had killed was in her dreams and she could not get him out. He was there all through the next day too, behind her eyelids, his face flashing up and then receding like the afterburn of a dying bulb. When she saw him he was no longer blind or dead. He was also younger, the lines wiped from his face, a hand raised towards her.

She had decided what she would do and there was no going back. It was easier for a boy. She had known this without being told. There was no mirror so she bent towards the water and used her reflection. There was blonde hair above her lip, on her chin. It came away, left her face smooth, red. Her hair was long the way her father had liked, past her shoulders, straggled. She cut the flotsam of it; what was left was short and ragged. The problem was, that even with the loose shirt it was clear what she had underneath. Not big or round but there all the same. Unavoidably so. She took the shirt off in a panic. The air was so cold it sucked into her belly, broke the breath out of her. She wrapped the cling film around her chest and then did it a second and a third time.

She walked on. A mooring rope stretched taut into the water and held on to a half-drowned boat. If she thought hard enough she would think herself away. She was four years old and spinning in the garden, arms out, the slices of world passing. She was ten, burying messages from next door in the soil. She was fourteen, picking the chillis out of the cake mix as Fiona dropped them in. She was sixteen and not the person she'd been before. She was sixteen and she needed a new name.

The Hunt

In the morning they all put their shoes on in a row at the door. Roger told me that they were going to the park and that I should help myself to anything I wanted from the fridge. Laura asked if I could do the washing-up. It was very quiet when they were all gone. I looked out the window. The garden was long and thin and the shed was at the end of it. I cut small slices of cheese from a block and fed them to Otto. I thought that I could hear you talking calmly from behind me. *We need to catch it*, you said *We're going to catch it.*

We're going to catch what? I asked, but there was no answer.

I hunted for and found the phone. It was one of the old-fashioned ones with dials rather than buttons. I rang the number for the office.

Gretel? It was the woman who ran the dictionary floor. Her name was Jennifer and there had always been an air of panic to her.

I'm sorry I've not called, I said. I've had an emergency and am going to need to take a couple more days off.

Down the other end of the phone there was silence.

Is that OK? I could hear her breathing. Jennifer? It'll only be a few more days.

There was a message for you, she said. I emailed you about it. Someone rang in the middle of the night when no one was here and left a voicemail.

Who left a voicemail?

I don't know. I rang the number but it was a phone booth. I thought that's why you were ringing.

Can you play it for me?

OK. I'm sure it's a prank. A joke. You know. I'll play it now.

There was a bang as she brought the ear of the phone against the speaker and then the sound of the automated voice counting the messages, the beeps as she moved through to the right one, the crackle as it began.

To start there was mostly quiet, background noise from outside the booth: a car or truck going past, footsteps on pavement, a clatter like rain or gravel beneath wheels. Then there was silence for so long I thought Jennifer must have made a mistake, turned the machine off or moved the earpiece away. I opened my mouth to say her name and then your voice spoke into my ear.

Gretel, you said. Gretel. I'm lost.

Otto was in the garden digging holes, but when he saw me he unearthed himself and flopped over. Beneath the scorched grass the ground was hard. There were posters for water rationing all over the neighbourhood but I could hear sprinklers coming from more than one direction. Inside I'd packed my bag, found the keys, ran as far as the car before I realised I still did not know where you were. Even you, it seemed, did not know that. I went to the shed and knocked both fists against the door, shouted and shouted until it was flung open. Even then I shouted for a moment longer, arms raised, head back. When I opened my eyes and saw her I realised that she was frightened of me. Good, I thought, I'm glad you are, I'm glad you're scared.

Fiona wouldn't let me go further than the threshold, bringing me back a cloudy glass of water which I pretended to drink. She had tiny wrists. There was a single bed with blankets and a gas stove with a pan. There was a stack of washed-out bean tins in the corner. Nothing else. She looked as if she'd been crawling through a mine, scrabbling to get out, starved of light. Not tall but hunched forward. She looked like one of the old women who bet on the horses in the shop around the corner from the office. I couldn't have pulled her eyes from her head if I'd hooked my fingers and tried to drag them out. There was thick, dark hair above her lip, between her eyes and from the tip of her chin. There was the smell of her living in there, barely leaving. Not unclean but overdone. I wondered if she showered at night using the outside hose – the way we used to on the river – the children peering at her through the window, the cold water falling over her upturned face. Or whether, perhaps, she sneaked in when everyone was asleep, bare-footed, mud prints left behind her, washing at the sink, raiding the fridge for anything out of date. She didn't look hungry, only as if she'd take what she could get. I knew the feeling.

Looking at her I understood, suddenly, why Marcus had been so obsessed with you. The way he'd follow you around or watch you carefully to see what you'd do, the way he listened so intently when you spoke. Roger and Laura had been right when they'd talked about that teacher; Marcus had been drawn to strong, older women. Marcus had loved Fiona and later he'd loved you, and there was never any other possibility for him than that.

I knew Marcus, I said.

I don't know any Marcuses.

The skin was wasting off her. I thought of the phone call, of what the woman at the stables had said about you turning up, disappearing. I was running out of time; I wanted to take her by the shoulders and shake her until everything she knew fell out.

When you knew her she was called Margot and you told her to leave, I said. Not long after that she appeared at the place where I lived on the river with my mother.

I moved further into the shed. She put the bed between us, her teeth clamped. I was beginning to understand that saying Margot's name to them was the same as saying yours to me: that ghost at my table, sitting there, eating all the food. The hair had thinned on top of her head and the scalp showed through.

I just want to know what happened. I realised that I had my hands up in the air. I brought them down slowly.

Why? she said.

Because it might help me find Marcus, Margot. I need to find her.

Why?

I looked at her. There was something about her face similar to a brick wall, smoothed over, gapless. She'd held on to her secrets for a long time.

Because, I said, I think my mother might be in trouble. I haven't seen her for sixteen years but I need to find her now and maybe Marcus will know where she is. Just tell me what you said that night.

You won't tell them? Her voice was wispy, underused. She turned both fingers so they were pointing at me and I understood that it was a threat.

You won't tell them, she said again.

I won't tell them.

She gazed at me. What do I get? she said.

What?

I've never told anyone. I've kept my secret. Why would I tell you? I need something in return.

I took out the money I had in my pocket, a couple of folded twenties, held them out to her.

She shook her head. What would I do with that?

I don't know what I can give you.

The same as I'm giving you. I want to know what happened. She was shaking a little.

What happened?

When you met her, when she stayed with you, what happened to her?

I don't remember much. I made myself forget most of it. I'm sorry.

She didn't say anything. I took a breath and told her about the river and the boat where I lived with you; about Marcus appearing one day with his tent and staying for a month. Talking, I realised that I remembered more than I thought; that the memories had been seeping back without my noticing them. I told her about playing Scrabble and reading the encyclopedia and making wind chimes and traps. About falling in love with Marcus in a childlike way, devoted, uncaring. I told her about you, your lessons from the encyclopedia, your sharp temper and long, wintery affection. We were afraid of something but I can't remember what it was, I said.

When I stopped I felt wrung-out, almost ashamed. Look at how the shape of you moved through anything of significance, eclipsing Marcus, even, nearly, me. Anyway, Fiona shook her head, dissatisfied.

What?

It's not enough, she said.

The River

New truths. Her name was Ben or Jake or Matthew. Her name was Leonard and she was a boy. Her name was Pierce or Johnny or Moses. Her name was Joe or David or Peter. She was not running away from home. She had not met a man called Charlie and killed him. Her name was Aaron or Brad or Martin or Richard. Her name was Alastair or Jack or Harry.

The river cut into the land. It was no good. She walked and walked until she slept. She saw the people on passing or moored boats looking at her and understood she did not look like a boy. She looked like something in between, uncertain, only half made. She looked like a girl who had killed a man and would carry it with her – in her pockets, in the corners of her mouth – for ever. She dropped her head to her chest, trudged on. At times the path grew so wild she had to force her way through, arms patterned with bramble cuts, the blood berry red against the brown bushes.

She passed through a town where there were boys riding their bikes, shouting and calling. Running men with long muscled thighs in bright green shorts.

Walkers who kicked dog shit into the hedge, dug in their pockets for chewing gum, their phones or keys. Old men in caps who drove their boats on warm days, drinking coffee and nodding hello. She wanted to find a body and movement that suited her. But she did not wear any of them well.

She wished him up. Wished him out from inside. A boy with her face and hands, a boy with Margot hidden at the back of him. A boy who had not killed a man. A boy who had no parents.

She copied the way they walked – these men – swinging her arms, setting her feet firmly on the floor. She watched them carefully, mimicked how they moved their mouths or laughed or spoke. She tried to conjure her own body to move the same way, tried to twist it, see it from the outside. She remembered the implied threat of the fishermen, thought of how Roger had smiled or that boy next door had frowned.

In the end she thought about the man on the boat, about Charlie. Remembered the way he'd moved – a little falteringly, otherwise certain – about the kitchen, reaching out for knives or cloves of garlic. Thought about the way he'd spoken, the riddles that had risen out of him. She closed her eyes, moved her legs, imagined what Charlie had been like when he was younger, not yet blind, leaping with confidence from the edge of the boat to the bank. It would be – she thought – a sort of memorial, a way of apologising. She reached down and pressed her hands into the damp earth. She felt Margot leaving. Stopped dumbstruck on the path, bent double. Felt a sudden, great sorrow at what was gone, what was left behind, what would never be spoken of again.

*

His name was Marcus. He did not remember his parents. He was walking along the canal. He had met and spoken to no one. He liked to run, to fish, to listen to riddles. He walked the way a boy walked, stopped and listened the way a boy would, spoke the way a boy would.

If anything had ever been laid out before it was not any more. The cling film was very tight around his chest, the sweat gathering in its creases. When he ran a palm across his face he thought he could feel the hair growing already, a little rough. He picked up a stone and tried to bounce it across the river the way he thought a boy might do. A boy would not worry about what he could not see in the water. A boy would not worry about what had happened on the boat. A boy would sleep without dreaming about Charlie's still, watchful face, looking up from the floor at him. The cold did not seem to bother him as much as it had. The hunger had become a distant threat, low in his belly. A boy would eat when food came to him, sparingly, rigorously. A boy would not find himself crying, hands curled around the gap where the tent pegs had been.

The Hunt

I rang the office again but there were no other messages. I used Roger and Laura's scanner and printed off fifty posters of your face with MISSING above it. I took them to the newsagents, the off-licences and petrol stations. I did not take them to the police station. What would I tell them? You'd been missing for sixteen years. I pulled over on a leafy residential street and left some on car windscreens. As I was doing so I realised the circular irony of this. Putting up posters of you where Roger and Laura must have put up posters of Marcus when all along he was with us, on the river. I knew that I would have to go there soon. It was the only place left to look and it was where I always thought of you as being. You were the messy river; you were the pines shedding bark in summer and the ground littered with my metal traps. I flipped a windscreen wiper up and slid a poster underneath. I was not ready to go back there yet.

The temperature hitched another notch and Roger proposed the pool. He had made coffee, which we drank sitting at the table. All the windows were open and Otto was splayed on the floor by my feet, tongue out.

I tried not to look at the shed. I was remembering more and more, but nothing that I felt was good enough to take to Fiona in exchange. I remembered being eight or nine and the kite you made me one feverish morning, your hair in braids and curls, the end of the string in your mouth. We'd taken it onto the roof of the boat and you'd stretched both arms above your head and launched it with a howl which seemed to carry it high, spiralling above us, tipping into the wind. I remembered your long silences, sometimes days without speaking while you lay on the bed or sat on the top of the boat and watched the current. Days that ended in screaming arguments, broken plates and swearing. Looking back I thought sometimes you were nasty for no reason but to stand your ground. That time you shaved all of our hair off. Or moments when you'd tell me how I was the same as you and that it was no good, it was no good for me to be that way. Change, you said. Think about it so hard that you become a different person's child. You were always talking about space, the order of the planets, the dog they sent up and that would never come back. This world was never good enough for you. You always thought there was more; you spent your whole life waiting for something more to come along.

Roger tapped my hand and said something.

What? Sorry.

You were miles away. I said, would you like to borrow a costume?

Actually I think I might stay here.

Really? It's a nice pool.

The truth is I'm a little afraid of water. I got up and refilled my coffee cup so I didn't have to look at him.

There was an awkwardness to being in someone else's house that I had not quite got used to. The day before I'd done my best to help out. I cleaned the kitchen and hoovered the living room. I did not attempt to cook but went to the local supermarket with a list drawn up in Laura's careful handwriting. *Milk, satsumas, toothpaste, nappies.* I sat on the sofa surrounded by small wriggling bodies and read whatever picture book I was given. The baby couldn't talk yet but the rest chanted along, mispronouncing or making up words entirely. Violet pressed beneath my arm and pushed her face against my chest. I can hear your thump. My what? She beat my pulse out onto my arm to explain.

I've never met anyone who's afraid of water, Roger said.

I hesitated. I had been entrusted with information about them that no one else knew. It seemed unfair to give him nothing. Knowledge had become something to barter there.

It's not bad. Not a phobia. I just avoid it when I can. I think it probably has to do with where I grew up. You know, by the river, where—

Where Margot went.

Yes. I remember some things. Mostly about my mother. And a little about the canal. And the day Marcus – Margot – arrived. But beyond that it's like a white-out. Have you ever had a white-out?

He snorted a sort of laugh.

Apologies. Whole parts of it are swamped away, submerged. I try and think of them and they aren't there.

Strange.

But I can see the tail end of them.

The tail end? He wrinkled his nose upwards. His face was very different from Marcus's, his mouth and eyebrows thin.

I can see things that I do or say, I explain. Problems that I have which trace back to there. I think being afraid of water is one of them. I think actually that something happened in the water. Maybe. I don't know.

Well you should come. It might stir it all up.

You mean make me remember?

You never know.

I put the balls of my feet against the kitchen tiles, which were a little cool. You know where she went now, I said. Don't you want to go there? See if she's still there. See, even if she's not, where it was she ended up?

He slid his cup across the table and then drew it back. We talked about it, he said. Laura said we should just go. There are friends who could look after the children for a couple of days. Laura thinks we would find her. Just there, waiting for us, not even a different age, certainly not a different gender. As if she'd been ... He seemed to struggle to find the right word. Crystallised.

You should go. I had pushed myself forward off my chair and was nearly standing. I've looked on a map. It's not far. It's not far at all. Even if she's not there. You can see it. Maybe you'll understand more. Find some sort of catharsis.

I wondered if I was so excited by the thought because I could help them or because they could go there instead of me, maybe even find Marcus and you and bring both of you back. I hoped it was the former but I was not so sure. I did not think selflessness came from living a life the way I had lived mine.

You don't understand, Roger said. We talked about it, but if she could come back she would have. We've been waiting. Where is she? It means something that she hasn't come home. She has a new life now or she's dead. Either way we're here if she wants to find us; we never left just in case she wanted to. He studied me. You must understand. Why didn't you look for your mother before?

I did look.

But you stopped?

Yes.

Why?

The same reason maybe. She didn't have to leave. She wanted to. I think it was in her blood somehow. But I think now she needs me to find her.

Well then. Let's go to the pool. You don't even have to get in if you don't want to. You can stand on the side. It'll do you good.

I thought that I would argue with him, but when everyone started gathering things – putting on flip-flops, filling bags – I gathered with them. It felt best that way. They were like an army, and I was, suddenly, inexplicably, swept along with them. I wished – out of nowhere, an abdominal feeling, almost painful – for a big family, too many for a normal car, a bus-full to carry me along in their wake.

At the swimming pool there was a pile-up by the vending machine and so I went into the changing rooms on my own. It was two in the afternoon, nearly empty. There was a naked woman in the shower. Maybe, when I was older, I would take up hobbies like this, a routine or structure, a comfortable life. There were no cubicles. I found an empty space, started to change. The suit I had borrowed from Laura was tight around the hips and bottom. I had put on weight. When I looked down I realised that this made me look more like you. I was not sure how I felt about that. As if the closer I physically came to finding you, the more I was becoming like you. Laura came in with all the children.

Gretel, Gretel, Violet said, you won't be allowed in if you don't shower.

I don't shower actually.

Ever?

Not ever.

I was given the baby to hold. He seemed to know I was no good for him and screamed himself purple and then was sick on my costume.

Now you'll have to shower, Violet said, seeming pleased with herself.

It was too late to go back. In the long window beside the pool I could see myself, blurred, a white-circled face and shapeless legs. The chlorine in the air burned the back of my throat. I did not know why I was there. The stairs up to the diving platform were reflected in the water. Violet was halfway up them: tiny-headed, bright green swimming costume, small insect limbs. Roger called her name. I could see Laura in the shallow end, bouncing with the baby. The roof spun until it was beneath my hands; the windows cracked and bellowed. I could hear the sluice that was near our boat thundering, the locks heaving open and closed. I could see you on the roof of the boat, arms in the air though there was no sign of the kite, your mouth open and shouting, the words taken and spun away before they reached me.

I did not see Violet falling but I heard the splash. She was a green, twisting smudge beneath the water. At the other end of the pool the blonde lifeguard was running. I put my toes over the edge and thought I saw something on the bottom, over beneath the metal steps in the corner. I was already stepping forward, dropping.

The water was colder than I'd expected. Violet was below me, sinking still. I kicked down towards her, eyes clenched open in the chlorine. There was movement by the metal steps. When I looked the Bonak was coming towards us, pressing off from the tiled floor, legs tucked in to its belly. Its throat was pale and heavy, its tail pendulumed behind it. It was prehistoric, cragged, dappled gold; beneath was a flash of white. Its long thoughtless face was turned towards us.

I grabbed Violet by the straps of her costume, bent my knees and pushed up with both feet. The surface seemed a long way off. I could see the fracturing of figures above, the colours of their clothes, their moving hands. The air burned all the way down. Violet was coughing, thrashing. Her hand connected with my nose. The water was patterned with blood. Someone was heaving me up; the edge of the pool scraped skin from my calves. The noise emerged in layers so I did not hear that the baby was screaming and that Laura was shouting until I was standing. I looked under the water for what I had forgotten, lingering by the steps or slinking along the bottom, rising, dragging itself along the shallow end, drawing close to us.

Four

Knock Knock Wolf

The Cottage

I decide that I will go mad if I don't work, that it is good for us to establish a structure, that we cannot go on this way for ever, and I tell you that for an hour every morning there must be quiet.

Quiet? you say, as if you've never heard the word before.

Yes, I say. Silence. There must, in fact, be silence. You can sit in the sitting room with me but I'm working so you have to sit quietly. In silence. You have to sit in silence.

You tip your head on one side. Working? You're only thirteen; you don't have a job, Gretel. You say it with such conviction I can think of nothing to reply and only hold my finger up warningly until you turn away, sidle to the armchair and sit down with your eyes closed.

I email Jennifer and she replies straight away telling me that she is glad to hear it. She gives me a word. An easy one: *extraordinary*. I make us a pot of coffee, pour you a cup and put it by your chair, sit at the desk. There is – for the first time in a week – calm. I put my head down and make sure not to look over at you. I can feel you watching me. I get out my index cards: white for citations, blue for production reference, yellow for drafted definitions. I drink some coffee.

*

When I first started working at the dictionary I was young and still thought of you often. You were inside me then in a way that faded as I grew older. I could still open my mouth and hear a sentence come out and know that it was there because I'd grown up with you. You'd made me and I wanted nothing more than to cut you out, cut you right out of my insides the way Alzheimer's did to a chunk of brain the size of an orange. You populated me; you ran the spirals of my thinking. I went to work, sat at the same desk every day, dreamed of something swimming in the River Isis, dreamed of your mouth moving around words I could no longer hear. I went to the same shop to buy a sandwich every lunchtime and – standing in the queue one day – I understood suddenly what you had done by creating your own language and teaching it to me. We were aliens. We were like the last people on earth. If – in any sense – language determined how we thought then I could never have been any other way than the way I am. And the language I grew up speaking was one no one else spoke. So I was always going to be isolated, lonely, uncomfortable in the presence of others. It was in my language. It was in the language you gave me.

I had done no work on *extraordinary* besides arrange the index cards. The small clock on the table says that two hours have gone. I want, suddenly, to tell you that I do not believe that any more, what I had believed standing in that queue. I do not believe that language rots through the brain and that I am the way I am because of the language you gave me. Nothing is laid out before us. Except, when I turn and look at the chair, you are gone. I should of course have known better, should have remembered you vanishing at the office, leaving on that bus. I look upstairs. The hot tap over the bath is on but the plug isn't in and you are not there. I turn the tap off. You have opened all of the windows on the top floor of the house so that the hot dust of dried earth comes in off the fields. When I look out the window of your bedroom I see you, halfway up the hill in the direction we sometimes walk, marching, arms switching back and forth. I go downstairs and out to the stone wall, shout your name. You wave an arm over your shoulder but do not turn.

Where are you going? I shout. You do not pause. I have spent my life chasing you. I almost go back inside, sit at the peaceful table and work. Stop, I shout and clamber over the wall and start up after you. It is too hot for chasing. You reach the top of the hill ahead of me and stop with your hands on your knees. I have one of those awful thoughts that swims up and that no one can ever know: it would be so simple if you had a heart attack. But you only rest for a moment and then move off, zigzagging. I branch across the field to catch up with you. Of course it is the water calling you. A shadow from passing clouds falls on my shoulders. I reach you by the jagged, nearly dried-up stream. You are grabbing at handfuls of the water and throwing them up towards your face. I sit down huffing beside you.

What are you doing? Why did you run away from me?

I was hot, you say in that tone you use that denies any retort. I bend next to you and scoop the water up. It tastes a little like iron, the bodies of factories, the inside of pipes. And when I glance up you have a strange look on your face – knowing, carefully considering, almost animal. Like one of those stray cats that sometimes found their way to us on the river and hung around until, just as quickly, they were gone.

The River

It became important only to keep going. The towns fell away. Marcus had not eaten for a day. When he dreamed of food it wasn't extravagant – slices of crustless bread, plain cake. It was no good. He built an iron box in his head and put in the whole plastic packet of bread, his parents with their glasses marks pressed into the ridges of their noses, Charlie, who'd cared for him before dying, Fiona's mouth moving with those awful, terrible words.

There continued to be signs of the canal thief. More dogs and cats had gone missing but also fish from lines and sheep from the small, nearly wild flocks that inhabited the banks. A couple of the boats he walked past were undergoing some sort of preparation: wooden boards nailed across the windows, broken bottles on string hung above the doors as a warning system. A woman followed for ten paces insisting he take care, would he take care? When he turned, panicked, stumbling, she gave him a knife and would not have it back again.

When he was out of sight he put the knife in his bag but did not feel better for it. Felt only that he now looked like someone who could have killed a man. For the rest of the day he sensed the dead man over his shoulder, following slowly after him, blindly listening to the sound of his footsteps to show him the way. He wanted to turn and tell him he hadn't meant it, it had been an accident. He wanted to drop into the water where it was still and quiet. Except the dead man was in the water, his long fingers, his open eyes. He walked on. The river was wild and curved.

The land opened up into an area of scrub: black bags of rubbish, an abandoned sofa, a fridge on its side. Beyond there was a gathering of straight-trunked trees. It was barely midday. He crouched, wincing, at a couple of the bags to see if there was anything inside, the smell enough to keep him going. To the left there was a sluice where the water ran hard and fast as a road. There was a sign on the wooden barrier but it was old, nearly gone, read only: DA G. He did not know what that meant; he did not care. There was enough open ground to get as far from the water as he'd been in days, in weeks. He knocked a fist against the side of his head to wake himself. He was so hungry that when he moved pitches of white stammered in front of his eyes. He would not think of the dead man, he thought. He would not think of him. Knocked a hand again against the side of his skull.

He dropped his bag and walked into the trees. Bent forward, looking. A couple of steps in there was a straggle of red berries and he put one in his mouth, held it on his tongue, spat it out. Dug a little at the base of some of the trees, not certain what he was searching for only that he needed to find it. I cannot walk any further, he thought. I cannot walk any more. Looking up he felt a great, rolling sense of relief. He would stop, just for a day. He would sleep and sleep.

He set the tent up. Sat in the entrance and peeled off his boots and socks. Blisters bulged on his skin. He smelled rancid. Never mind. He was so tired he couldn't tell the difference between parts of his body. He dozed, drifting off and then coming back to his cold, bare feet on the mud, head jerking off his chest. He opened his rucksack and hunted, found a few stray breadcrumbs, ate them off his fingers. Slept a little more. Behind his eyelids there were dreams of the dead man, the boat growing out of his arms, the stench of burning lamb. The dead man put one amber eye very close to his and when it blinked Marcus came awake, fumbling up, shouting.

There was a girl crouched not far away. Crow-headed, pink tights streaked with muck, fingers dug into the dirt, unblinking eyes. He yelled, crabbed backwards into the tent.

The girl rose, wiped her hands on her tights. Her clothes were too small for her, lines of pressure at wrists and ankles. Her mouth was open. Just beyond her was his rucksack, which she'd dragged out and opened, rifled through. When she came closer he saw she was holding the book he'd taken from the dead man's boat when he left.

You won't like it, he said so loudly he heard his own voice crash back from the trees.

She shook the book at him and scowled. Her face was squarish; eyebrows coming together in the middle in a long line of disapproval. He did not know what to do. He folded his sleeping bag into a tight ball, did up the buttons on his coat, put his boots back on. He wanted so badly not to walk again, to sit, to sleep, to never move. The girl sneezed and wiped her nose upwards on her hand. Crawled a couple of paces closer. She was very near, holding something out to him. It was a hank of bread. A wave of panicked joy swelled over him. He put it in his mouth so fast he almost choked, chewed awkwardly. She held out the book. As if some kind of deal had been made without his realising or agreeing to it.

They sat on the ground in front of the tent. She was covered in a thin film of dirt, as if she'd been dug out of the earth. There was, it was true, something root- or bulb-like about her, knobbly knees, limbs bursting from her clothes. She scratched the thick tufts of hair around her ears with one hand. Her pockets bulged at her sides.

He opened the book and he read to her. The font was small and difficult to read. He did not know a lot of the words on the page. Next to the riddles were strange, spindled drawings of misshapen creatures with the head of one animal and the body of another. In one of the pictures he could see the barn that had been in the riddle the dead man had told him that first day.

You won't like this, he said again, but I'll read it if you want me too. If you have more bread somewhere? She didn't answer.

I don't think you'll like it, he said. He did not, he realised, want her to leave.

Except she did like it. Her mouth moving around the words, pointing, demanding: this one again. And he'd read it more slowly, faltering. Often there were words he could not say which she spoke with ease. Leaning forward, pressing a mud fingerprint against it, spelling it out. The words seemed to come easily to her, as if she were inventing them. Each time she would look up at him, pleased as punch, the soft curl of her wide mouth, the flash of yellow teeth. *What can travel around the world while staying in one corner? The more you take the more you leave behind.*

Halfway through one she got up and he watched her hastening away, arms pumping as she ran. When he retrieved his bag he saw what she had taken: two pairs of underpants, the empty bread bag, two shirts. There was a page torn out jaggedly from the riddle book.

He crawled back into the tent and put his head down against the hard floor. He keened for what he had lost, for what he had given away, for what he had done. He could feel his parents, somewhere down the river. They were looking for him or they were not. They were at the round kitchen table, reaching for a cup or turning the page of a newspaper or swinging the front door open, just about to step out. He wanted, very badly, for them to find him. He wanted to tell them why he had gone, why he had done it. It would be fine then. If they understood. They would pass out of each other's spheres, never think of one another again. They were sitting at the round kitchen table, and the dead man was there too, looking up at him.

The things Fiona had said he would do were tangled up, rolled around the tent. They were the colour of skin, dry and scaly. They crawled up the front of his chest, popped inside his mouth. His cheeks bulged in an effort not to say them. Not to say what Fiona had said he would do to his father. Do to his mother. With his mother. Woke sweating through the sleeping bag, rearing up.

The Hunt

I bought a bottle of wine and sneaked it down the side of the house to the shed. Fiona opened the door enough for me to see only a slice of face. I've remembered something, I said. She let me in. We drank steadily out of tea cups. She smacked her lips together, rubbed her stomach with one hand.

On the way back from the swimming pool I'd remembered more and more, the trickle turning into a flood. There were still gaps – huge holes the size of train tunnels – but there was also a shape, a story.

Well, she said, slurping wine noisily. You'd better tell me then.

I don't think you'll be able to understand.

She put her cup down onto the floor with a click, lifted her legs up onto the bed and rested them there. I could hear Otto outside, snuffling around, the sound of the television from a nearby house.

You know, she said, the first time I ever saw something that wasn't there I was a boy and I was watching the bulls get castrated on the farm my parents owned. My sisters weren't allowed but my father took me. I always wondered why he did that. I was so shy I could barely ask for the salt.

The men who did the castrating came in from the local town. The bulls were young and scared and I felt so strongly for them. They got through twenty in an hour. My father held my hand and we were close enough to study what had been cut away. They were like strange plants.

She picked up the cup again and raised it in a sort of salute.

When I looked away from all those cut testicles I saw someone in the corner of the barn, standing beneath one of the hay hatches. It was me but I was a woman. That's the first time I knew something was going to happen before it did.

She drained the rest of the cup and then nudged me to pass the bottle. I smelled myself as I moved: chlorine and sweat.

Are you going to tell me or not?

Yes, I said. I've remembered what we were afraid of. I took a big breath. I did not know if it was a good idea to tell her; to say it out loud. It seemed madness to speak it there, in a tiny shed at the end of a garden.

We called it the Bonak, I said. That's what we called everything we were afraid of, but we were most afraid of this. I saw it in the pool. Swimming towards me. It was a creature, an animal. It was big. I saw it in the water.

A creature?

Yes.

I waited for her to laugh or tell me to leave, but she did not. I felt suddenly exhausted, as if I'd run a marathon or swam for days. I did not tell her what else had started coming back: a trap, a fishing rod, the glass of the roof hatch beneath my elbows.

What happened to it? she said.

I wondered if she believed me. I was uncertain if I believed myself or had only, accidentally, made up something that could not possibly be true. There were rules – *the universal force of attraction between all matter; oxygen is a colourless, odourless, tasteless gas essential to all living organisms* – and what I was proposing did not fit into the rules as we understood them. Something that big, in the water, taking children, killing dogs. I wondered if – if I'd remembered it right – it had even been true then. Or if we'd somehow brought it into being. I could not decide which prospect was worse.

I think my mother killed it, I said. Fiona had tipped back in her chair so the front legs hovered off the floor and she didn't seem to be listening. I saw, looking, that she had rearranged the shed, thrown away the tower of bean tins, made the bed. It had not occurred to me that while I was going over old days she was too, that she might have reached a conclusion herself. She drew her shoulders up like the handles of a bag.

I'm in need of a good meal, she said. Lunchtime tomorrow should do it. I'll tell you what I saw.

The River

The girl in the pink tights was called Gretel Whiting, and the next day she stayed until it got dark. He got used to her. How she rambled, ran without warning. Where's the fire? she'd say and cackle. Often she talked to herself more than to him, chattering. Marsupial, she said. Gratitude. Longitude. She had a holey plastic bag which she called a sprung, and when the wind dropped low enough to hear the river she cupped a hand over her ear. Do you hear? The messin?

I forgot, she said and, digging into a pocket, brought out a crumbled piece of cake. Do you like it?

Yes, he said. It was soft and porous, streaked with oil from her fingers. He was so relieved she was there that he followed her wherever she went. He had not realised how lonely he'd been, how long the days were. He worried that she would leave suddenly, without warning, and then the hours would be years again and he would mostly just be scared. Her hair was forced into an uneven plait poking from her collar which made him think that she must belong to someone.

Where are your parents? he asked.

My mother's a sealady, she said. She's got fins for feet and gills. She's flighty through the water.

What does that mean?

It means she's a mermaid.

That's not true, he said, though uncertainly.

Come on, let's go this way. She looks like you and me, she said. She can breathe underwater; she knows every single word in the world, she's an archaeologist and a surgeon and very famous to everyone. I call her the doctor or S. She calls me El or Hansel though she won't tell me why. She can dig from one side of the world to the other and has done many times, she doesn't need to sleep, she can eat animals whole, she says she's a runner-away but really she's a stayer-putter and very good. Gretel drew a breath. Also, she said, she can cook really well.

He followed slowly. He could hear the river behind them. He trusted it less when he couldn't see it. What was stopping it climbing the land like the ground was just a ladder? Gretel clambered on top of a downed fridge. Her hat was pulled low to her eyes, scarf over her nose, a tangle of mitten strings. The mist caught around her face and cut off whole slides of her body. Objects swum out of it, seemed to move where before they'd been stationary. He wanted to ask her more about her mother, about the lies or truths she'd told about her but—

Over there, she called. Pointing off somewhere. The bits and bobs. They're over there.

She didn't walk but skittered, jumping from one point to another. He followed the sound of her voice calling back to him. She liked, it seemed, his name. Drew it out into its disparate parts: Mar-ca-s. Or made up nicknames: Marie, Carcass, Ram. When he caught up with her she had an object made of wire in her hands. She levered the mouth of it open.

What is that?

She ignored him. We must find them all, she said. They were traps, and inside them were mostly field mice, a couple of ancient-faced frogs, some river rats which were big and which he didn't like. She let most of them go and they crawled away, dragging themselves along. The animals that were already dead she gathered up. He was given a small fat mouse to carry and he put it in his pocket and tried to forget it was there. When they were done she re-baited the traps using scraps of meat, rinds of pork that he wished she would give to him instead.

I'm trying to catch something big, she said. He thought about the canal thief, about the lure Charlie had been making before he died.

Like a fox? he said.

She shrugged.

Like a badger?

She scowled. Like a Bonak.

He felt his stomach drop a little as if they'd passed, without moving, over a hill. What's a Bonak?

He watched her heaving the mechanism back down, snapping it into place.

It's anything, she said, gritting her teeth.

What do you mean?

Last summer it was this stupid dog that was so hungry Sarah said it would bite. But ages ago it was a storm that nearly wrecked the boat and another time it was a fire that burned a lot of the forest and that we thought would burn us too. This winter it's something else. Sarah says maybe it's the worst Bonak there has ever been but we don't know yet.

It's what you're afraid of?

It's the Bonak, she said simply and wouldn't talk about it any more. She held up a trap for him to look closer at. When he asked her how they worked she only pointed to various parts, chattering a little to get all her words out. And then this bit, and then this bit here, and afterwards. Do you see?

They were back at the edge of the river without him realising they'd circled round. The ground cracked beneath his boot. His lungs hurt from the cold. She showed him one of the metal objects hanging from the river bushes.

Flimflam, she said. Wind chime. Wouldn't let him touch.

He stood and watched her threading the captured creatures down onto the spokes so that they hung with their bellies towards the water. The mud at the edge of the bank was thick, almost red; he watched his boot sinking in.

Listen, she said, holding a hand up towards his mouth. They stood still. The wind came down the river, parting the banks of fog and moving through the chimes so that they seemed to sing. She speared a dead frog through its belly. He wondered if it was some kind of protection against the water, against the current, against the canal thief, the Bonak.

It doesn't mean anything though, he said and, even wrapped up, he could see her anger; her eyebrows creasing, her mouth twisting upwards. She turned the nearest wind chime until it spun of its own accord. He thought about her mother swimming in the river without needing to go up for air or stop to sleep. He thought about the strange relief of telling someone what he had done on the boat, how his hands couldn't close properly because he still felt he was holding the tent pegs clenched in them. He thought about her mother digging through the core of the earth, staying put and leaving all at once, eating animals whole.

He was in love with Sarah before he even met her.

The Hunt

The restaurant called itself Chinese but there was chips and macaroni cheese on the menu along with the spring rolls and chow mein. It took us nearly an hour to walk up the hill to the centre of town. Fiona skirted the sun, keeping to the shadows. I wanted to ask her when she had last left the garden. I didn't. When I offered her my arm she straightened and looked down her nose at me, affronted.

We were the only people in the restaurant. There were red paper lanterns hanging from all the windows, a fish tank with carp the size of my forearm, a hole through which we could see the chef smoking and watching television. Now was not the time for polite conversation. We held menus in front of our faces. Occasionally I sneaked glances at her but she was engrossed, blue-veined fingers curved around the red leather menu, tongue probing thoughtfully across the top of her mouth. I was reminded of that time with you: the plate of raw meat you'd forced down, the wine glass tipping like a telescope towards your face, the condom smeared around your knife. In that moment Fiona was – I think – happy in a simple, uncomplicated way that you would have dismissed. She moved her chopsticks around, looked at the design on her plate.

She held the menu up so I could see and pointed things out to me. I was suddenly glad that I brought her here, even if nothing came of it, even if she told me nothing. It had been easy to imagine being Roger or Laura, waiting and waiting; the woman who'd sent Margot away living in their shed. Here I saw that it was worse to be Fiona, that she had been waiting too. Waiting for someone she could tell, for someone she could explain it to. Waiting to become something other than the person who made their child leave.

The waitress was, give or take, fourteen. I ordered prawn crackers.

What is a Bacardi Breezer? Fiona said.

The waitress brought her a bright orange bottle and both of us watched her taste it. She blinked at me. Drank it down. Asked for another.

I didn't know what I was doing but Fiona seemed in her element; ordered enough for a party. To start: char siu BBQ pork buns, beef stomach in black bean, dumplings, and salt and pepper squid. A whole fried sea bass topped with soy minced pork and diced water chestnut sauce; beef tripe with glass noodles and Chinese leaf in a pot, bean sprouts with salted fish and dan dan noodles. We did not bother with rice but Fiona wanted some chips. The waitress went back over the order slowly. In the kitchen the chef turned off the television.

Fiona ate all the prawn crackers and then waved the bowl for more. When she was on her third Bacardi I ordered a glass of wine. The food came whenever it was ready, great plates overflowing onto the paper tablecloth. There was something blissful about the way she went about it, eating straight from the serving platters, trying one and then the other. Everything was spicy with an aftermath burn that made me sweat and then weep, my nose running. Fiona took off the tweed coat which she'd insisted I borrow from the house for her despite the heat. Underneath she was wearing a red dress with lace sleeves and a long skirt. When the chef had finished cooking he leaned through the hatch to watch us. We worked steadily, not decreasing in speed. The dumplings were thick. The pork had a layer of fat which had burned to crackling. The dan dan noodles had hidden caverns of mince buried beneath them. I gave up on the chopsticks, asked for a fork.

She began to rest between mouthfuls, observing me through half-lidded eyes, the sleeves of the dress rolled up over her forearms. I was concentrating so intently on the food that I almost missed the first thing she said.

What? I swallowed my mouthful so fast I nearly choked.

I knew what she was going to do. So I sent her away.

What did you know?

She picked up the last of the dumplings with her fingers and after she had eaten it she told me.

The River

Gretel had come to see him again and brought a piece of bread so hot it burned the top of his mouth and some kind of hard cheese crusted with grains of salt. The game she wanted to teach him was called Knock Knock Wolf and this was how it went. They found the best tree in the wood. He was to stand in front of it and knock twice with his fist, wait a moment, say knock knock wolf and then turn. She was ten paces behind him. The aim of the game, she said, was to get so close she could touch him without his ever seeing her move.

Knock knock?

Knock knock wolf. Ready?

I think so, he said.

Go. The game, she'd said, was a duvduv one, which he thought meant something good, that she really liked. There were protective headphones with yellow cups that she wore on her ears like muffs. She slumped her shoulders in a motion he was coming to know as her exaggerated annoyance move. It was easier not to think of the dead man when she was there.

Go.

He turned back to the tree. Closed his eyes, held his breath. There was a slowing down, the cold against his face. He could hear the sound of the river and, beneath that, the slow crunch of pine needles under Gretel's feet, birds moving further into the wood. He waited as long as he could stand it – not long – and then blurted the words out. Turned. He could feel his pulse in his mouth

Gretel was on one foot, frozen five steps away, unblinking, arm over her head. He watched her but she did not move. He turned back to the tree.

Knock knock wolf.

She was closer again. One arm stretched forward, head turned to the side as if looking at something off to the left. He followed her gaze – there was nothing there but the grey winter scrub grasses – and when he looked back she'd taken another step – just a small one – sidling nearer. He swung round, fell over the words, swung back. She was grinning now, yellow-toothed, the muffs abandoned, both arms hovering up towards him. He turned back and a moment later – halfway through the words – felt her hand, surprisingly strong, gripping his shoulder, her sharp exclamation of achievement.

It's a good game, she said as he turned. She was jigging on the spot, one knee high and then the other, wrists shaking in the air. It's a good game, a good game, a good game.

Yes, he said. Though he wasn't so sure, thought perhaps he preferred reading the book or even trailing her as she emptied the traps. There was a hysterical, clenching fear to it that he did not enjoy. He did not like having his back turned to the water; nor waiting for that inevitable hand. More than that, he did not like the thought that perhaps it would never come. He might stand there for hours and, finally turning, realise that it had been a ruse all along and that she was gone. Or – worse – that there was someone else standing there quietly, the dead man, following after all.

They played it again and then again. He got better at gauging direction by sound, saying the words fast and turning as he said them, thinking he'd almost caught her, though each time she was still, not even wavering.

Shall we swap over? he said after the third time, but she only shook her head. He turned to the tree. Counted a couple of seconds, said the words and then looked back at her. She was standing on one leg and was craning, again, over to the left. He looked too. There was the fridge on its side, the lumpy bin bags moving a little in the wind, beyond that a patch of nettles. He knew – because he'd walked the whole area – that the nettles went on for a few paces and then the land grew soft and the river began. He could see nothing but that.

What are you looking at?

She didn't answer.

Is there something there? We don't have to keep playing if you've seen something.

She didn't even wobble. The canal thief. Except she didn't say anything. He looked back to the tree, counted barely two seconds – fast – shouted the words and twisted just as he felt the hand on his shoulder, the shock of it propelling him forward so his legs got caught around each other, and he fell, calling out, already trying to scrabble away. Nearby he could hear Gretel laughing in that way she had, loudly, harshly. When he looked up the sun was so bright he could see only the silhouette of the person above him, a shaded outline with a wide hand reaching out of it and down towards him.

You, she said, must be Marcus.

Five

The Dead Man Moving in the Forest

The Cottage

What comes back to us from that long-lost trailing river – a spine against the backbone of the country? What did we summon up there? A wildish girl and her wilder mother, living like demons or animals out where no one could get to them. Look at us now. Faded, wretched, bent on destroying one another or ourselves, rattling around in a cottage not big enough to hold the two of us. You remind me, at times, of Fiona. The way she'd eaten with that desperate, grasping hunger; the way the story she'd been keeping secret had squirmed through her and made her mad and lonely and frightened. The way that Marcus loved you both with a great love that never did him any good. But I love you, you say to me in the supermarket, and I want to say it back but I can't, not yet; I can't give you that. And I want to tell you that I think we made it. Whatever it was that pressed through the calm, cold waters that winter, that wrapped itself around our dreams and left its clawed footprints in our heads. I want to tell you that it might never have been there if we hadn't thought it up.

The River

The woman reminded Marcus a little of a doctor he'd had when he was younger and who'd been unsmiling and rarely spoke. She'd shown him an X-ray of his insides: the pods of dark and white, the hard skeins in among the caverns. He'd mistrusted her for it, being able to see the way she did. This woman was smaller than him and had moles up and down her arms, on her face; her hair was very dark and her eyebrows met in the middle the same as Gretel's. She used her eyes the way the machine that had taken the X-ray did. He felt them cutting in.

The boat they lived on was moored just around the corner from Marcus's tent and was green and orange with rust and mould. It was different from Charlie's; had no windows, only a roof hatch through which the light fell, dappled, onto a pile of sheepskin and tartan blankets; buckets of dirty dishes, a stove with a gas fixture, piles of books and crockery. On the counter there was a bowl from which she took out and peeled an egg, gave it to him. He put it into his mouth and then did not know where to look. Looked at her boots, which were heavy and clogged with mud.

I was going to make some food, she said in a way that made it unclear whether she was inviting him to stay or not. Gretel grabbed his hand and towed him up the steps and outside.

Is that your mother? he asked her quietly so the woman in the boat couldn't hear. Gretel was on tiptoe pulling at a fish that was starting to rot on one of the wind chimes.

That's my mother, she said loudly. Her name's Sarah. She said that she wanted to meet you. She said that she was very interested to meet the boy with the book.

The boy with the book?

That's you. She calls you that or the boy in the tent or the quiet.

The quiet?

I told her you didn't talk much and she said you sounded like quiet itself. She says things like that sometimes.

They made the rounds of all the traps and wind chimes, and by the time they came back Sarah was out on the roof, legs dangling off the side. She had a cast-iron pan in one hand – the steam rising, blackened bacon inside – a cigarette in the other. Gretel ran up and wrapped her arms around her neck.

Watch out, El, she said. Do you want one? she said to him.

What?

She nodded her head so the cigarette in her mouth bobbed up and down. A cigarette. Do you want a cigarette?

No, thank you.

Suit yourself.

He didn't know what to do with his arms and legs. When he moved he felt as if he wobbled ridiculously. She was wearing a thin white T-shirt with the straps of a swimming costume visible underneath, a silk skirt that she tucked around her thighs and balanced the rim of the skillet on as she smoked. Her mouth was very wide and the bottom lip was heavy. He did not think she was older than his parents, but then, besides Fiona, he did not know anyone who was. Not for the first time he wished that he was decked out better; knew instinctively what to do and say. She smoked slowly, tugging the cigarette from her mouth or simply blowing the smoke out around it. When she was done she picked a piece of bacon out of the hot pan and ate it. He could see the grease on her fingers and – when she wiped them – on her knees, which were brown as river water.

Here.

He took a piece of bacon out of the pan. Gretel took two and ran before anyone could stop her. He turned and watched Gretel rushing away into the treeline. When she was gone he was very aware of the shape of spaces: the square between him and Sarah, the triangle of Sarah's legs hanging against the damp side of the boat, the empty air in his open hands.

Tell me about yourself, she said. Marcus, right? Do you have a swan song?

A what?

What would you say about yourself if you were going to die right at this moment?

He felt a great, panicked stillness fall over him. He was certain she could see on his face everything that had happened: the reason he had left; what he'd seen or heard on the river; what had happened with Charlie; why he could never go back.

I'm just walking, he said eventually, choking the words out. He felt as if she'd reached inside his chest and pressed everything out of place. He had never felt this before and he was uncertain what it meant. She looked very like Gretel: one of her eyes a little wider than the other, her pupils the colour of steel.

Walking where? Walking to what?

Just. Just walking.

Just walking? That sounds good. Just walking with nowhere in mind? That sounds duvduv.

Yes, he said. He was a little undone by the way she repeated his words, spoke them back to him with that questioning rise at the end. Maybe.

I think we'll leave soon, she said. She'd turned her body towards the river. Head downstream. See what we can find. She seemed, he thought, not really to be speaking to him. He felt as if he was listening in on something he should not listen in on.

I get impatient sometimes, you know? She twisted back to look at him. He felt the broad span of her gaze, sinking into skin, burying in.

Yes, he said. Although he did not.

We've been here since Gretel was born. It's a long time to stay in one place. Sometimes I just want to ... She didn't finish her sentence, only lifted her arms above her head and pressed them upwards as if breaking through an invisible barrier.

They sat at the small table to eat. Gretel talked very fast and dropped the soup Sarah had made down her front. He was so hungry he funnelled his spoon up steaming, blistered the roof of his mouth.

More?

Yes, please.

Sarah refilled his bowl. She had eaten little, smoked another cigarette. For someone so small she seemed – much as Gretel did – to take up a lot of room. She sat on the bench with one bare foot up next to her, an elbow on the table, leaning back. He ate again, felt his belly cramping around the unexpected food, more than he'd had since Charlie had died.

We read the encyclopedia, don't we? Gretel said.

Yes, said Sarah.

This morning we read about the Minotaur. Do you know what that is, Marcus? It's a creature with the body of a man and the head of a bull and it lives in a maze. Which made me think, actually, about the panopticon. Do you know what that is?

You are going to choke if you don't slow down, Hansel, Sarah said. And I am not going to perform the Heimlich manoeuvre on you.

Well. It's the perfect prison because there is only one watchman, but the people who live in the prison cannot tell whether they are being watched or not so they act as if they are always being watched even if they're not. Mum said it runs on self-imposed paranoia. I don't know about that but it made me think, actually, about the Bonak.

He put his spoon back into his bowl. When he looked up Sarah was watching him again. He wished he didn't feel so nervous every time she did that. His tongue felt too large for his mouth, he could feel the click his breathing made as it came out of his throat.

You've heard about it? Sarah said. You know about the Bonak.

I don't know, he said.

You've come from up the river, haven't you? From the north. We've been hearing rumours about it from that direction for weeks.

What is it?

Gretel tapped his arm but didn't say anything.

It's probably nothing, Sarah said and piled the soup bowls on top of one another. People on the river have always been superstitious. The water has a way of making anything that was clear murky. You think I haven't seen things out there? When it's misty or on days so hot the air gets wavy I think I've seen things I left behind, never thought I'd see again. I've seen a thin man walking between the trees or an animal with the face of a woman or something worse. A person can convince themselves of anything out here. River people aren't like other people. You won't see the police down here. You won't see child services or priests. River people don't use mirrors; they don't like to be on the ground too long. So. It might be nothing.

It was the most he'd heard her speak and he felt a little stunned, couldn't think of anything to say.

But we're keeping an eye out, Gretel said. Aren't we?

Yes. We are.

Midnight, back in the tent, it caught up with him, soused over him. Chucking the sleeping bag away, sitting up in the five-fathom-deep dark. He muffled the sound of his crying in his wrist, wet-armed now, tugged at the cling film, which had become tangled, brushed his hand over the stubble that was growing from his chin. Listened for a moment for the dead man moving in the forest. Nothing.

The Hunt

The night after my meal with Fiona there was an email. There was no subject heading and you had not written my name or answered with yours. Still, I knew it was from you. You might as well have reached both arms out of the screen, put your hands around my neck.

I am on the river. I have found him.

You were with Marcus, you must be. I thought of telling Roger and Laura, of taking them all with me. Except what if you were wrong? What if you were mad? What if you hadn't found him at all?

I borrowed a tent and a sleeping bag. I wanted to leave Otto behind but he followed me, banked on his hindquarters, bared teeth pitted with holes.

Stay. Stay. He lunged, tried to bite.

Before leaving I stood with Roger and Laura in the kitchen and asked what they would do now. The door to Fiona's shed was open in the heat and there was the beat of music coming from inside, electronic and fast. Roger balanced the baby on the table and it tried to roll for the edge, heaving one arm over its hip to gather momentum. It seemed impossible to me that they could stay there. A change had occurred. I could see it on their faces and in the way they moved. I had – without meaning to – made Margot alive to them, reanimated her. For a long time they had seen nothing but the door closing behind her, but now they knew where she had gone and could imagine her there. Laura shrugged and went out into the garden.

She's angry with me, Roger said.

Why?

She thinks I've given up.

I pulled the zip closed on my borrowed bag. I was leaving the car with them. I had things which Margot – leaving in the night, scared – had not: a map, enough food to last me the trip there and back.

Have you?

He opened his hands to encompass the small house, the children rolling in a ball down the slide while Laura shouted for them to be careful, the baby straining with the effort of trying to turn its heavy body, the sink full of plates from the meal the night before. What's wrong with giving up?

I stood looking at him and thought maybe he was right. Maybe it would be fine if I didn't find you after all. He smiled a little, turned the tap on over the dirty dishes.

Can I ask you a question? I said.

That very much depends on the question.

We were afraid of something that winter. My mother and me. Margot too. We thought it was taking children and that it had come for us. We called it the Bonak.

The Bonak?

It was a word we made up when I was really young. We made up a lot of words, but that's the one I remember the best. It meant a lot of different things over the years but it was always whatever we were afraid of.

A long list on a boat on the river, I'm sure.

Yes.

I was a frightened child, he said. Not like this lot. They're afraid of nothing.

What were you afraid of?

He gestured again outwards. You name it. Under the bed, in the wardrobe, cars, fish bones, the swing going over the top at the playground. They became an amalgamation at one point, I remember now, of everything my parents had warned me about.

You made yourself afraid? You created a monster.

In a way.

That, I said, is what I wanted to ask you. The more I remember the more it's only snatches, fragments of things that I know at the time felt enormously important. We believed things.

He turned back towards me. You want me to tell you if you created the Bonak you saw that winter? You and your mother and Margot.

Yes. Do you think we did? Talked it into being?

I don't know if it matters, he said, and I watched his face as he thought of Margot. I thought of her too: her close-cut hair, her anxious face turned towards us while the end of the year drew in.

At the door Violet had begun to scream, not crying but bellowing. I wondered if she would have strange, distorted memories of me when she grew up. A woman who came to stay for a week one summer and then was gone. As

I walked away Otto ran ahead, yelping and skidding his ungainly nose on the ground. I felt the same way. It was good for there to be no one but us again. Even if we were going back to the river. I realised, as I reached the canal, that I'd not said goodbye to Fiona. Maybe it was for the best. I thought of the fork heavy with food moving towards her mouth, the tablecloth ripping beneath her arms, her mouth moving. I thought of what she'd told me.

The summer after the boy Fiona saw the bulls castrated he began trying on his sisters' clothes. Sneaking back into the house while everyone was at school or working. He would put on their dresses and study himself in the wardrobe mirror, push his feet into their too-small shoes. Hours were sucked into the caverns of red lace, blue suede, silk and leather. How much did they notice? His anxious parents, kicking their boots off at the door, eating toast on the go. That he had stolen his mother's razor and shaved off all the traitorous body hair? That he dreamed of castration, the cool walls of the shed, the door rattling closed on its runners, the testicles popping like peaches?

There were male years. Too much time to count. They were not worth noting. He did not tell his parents what he was going to do. He left and knew that he could not go back. Part of him was still there, in his old, narrow bed or running to the top field to rescue a straying calf. In the city he would have a new name and a different face.

Five or so years into womanhood she'd caved, written her parents a letter without signing it. She wrote, *I am living in the city. People who walk past me on the street do not think I am a man. Yesterday someone called me madam in a bakery. Did you know before I did and just lack the language to explain?* Her parents would never reply and she would not blame them. They were not the sort of people who would have taken the time to write to a stranger. She was not the boy who'd sat cautiously at their table, his feet barely touching the floor, his hands hovering a few inches above the wood. She did not send anything to them again though at times she would write as if she meant to. She wrote, *I have a job at a supermarket. I do not like it but it is paying the rent. I do not know yet how to talk to people so I am mostly on my own. I do not think of you or the farm or the others. It has been nearly a decade since I last saw you and nothing you remember about me exists any more.*

Something else. A change separate from just that of her becoming a woman. Small things at first: reaching a hand to catch a cup before it fell, taking out an umbrella even though it was a warm day. Later it became clearer. Avoiding certain streets or shops, taking different routes when she was out walking, not wearing a skirt whose zip she knew – though she did not know how – would break that day. It was not, she came to realise, second sight, rather more a knowing. As if parts of her brain were hollow like sea caves and occasionally became full with knowledge that had not been there before.

She had seen the small house in an estate agent's window and liked it, gone in to ask and come out certain she would have it. She was tired of running through a different city every month, riding trains, watching out. There would be a certainty to a house. She would paint the stairs yellow, the bathroom green. She had no furniture but she had seen herself there, drinking a glass of wine on the step to the garden, levering open the stiff windows.

A week or so after she moved in a man came round with banana bread, said he lived next door and if she needed anything she should ask. He was owlish in his glasses and moon face, his holey jumper. She'd made them both a sandwich. He'd asked her to dinner, and she'd felt then the itch of something she was unable, yet, to identify. The familiar feeling of a knowledge that did not belong to her worming its way in. She studied him carefully as he finished his sandwich and washed up the plate – without asking – in her sink. What was it? What did she see looking out of his face? He told her about Laura, the woman he loved, and their daughter who was called Margot and who was enamoured with her.

Enamoured with me? I haven't met her.

He led her out into the garden and pointed to a window of the house next door where there was, for a moment, a face looking out.

She's been watching you, I'm afraid. She was supposed to bring the bread herself but she got scared.

Fiona could see the gaps ahead of him, the spaces he would fall into. She did not know yet what they would be, only that they would be there. She told him she would love to come for dinner.

Their domesticity calmed her. She went to their house for meals often, read to Margot at the table. She forgot, more and more, what it was she had sensed that first day, the reason she had allowed them to befriend her at all. She cooked awful, extravagant meals in their small kitchen, let Margot plant courgettes in her garden. They celebrated birthdays together with an ease which surprised her. They were not her family; they were not her blood. Margot drew stick drawings in which Fiona towered over the rest of them, her hands as big as spades, her mouth a wide smiling arc.

There was a bad year. There had been bad ones before and she had not yet the knack of telling when they would come, rising out of the decades like sores. She had dates in the diary for seeing Laura and Roger that she missed because she was skipping days, waking up and finding that she'd lost a week and had no idea how she'd spent it. She would come to in the bathrooms of coffee shops, on buses, in rooms she had never been in before. Time was refracting, loosening, was weak as clay.

She shuffled tarot cards in the back rooms of shops or made a little money out of predicting wins at the races, though she – just like everyone else – was liable to be wrong just as often as right. She picked pockets, robbed a couple of houses, spent some nights in jail. She missed the rent and did not go back to the house. She slept beneath bridges, in doorways, on buses. She slept at train stations, predicted delays and cancellations weeks before they happened, watched the steady carriages coming in, the same people getting on and off.

It got worse. Days did not run straight but ducked forward, swanned back. She came to realise that – all along – nothing she predicted was without consequence. Mugs she had caught before they could fall smashed in her hands hours later; umbrellas broke in the middle of rainstorms so heavy she thought she would be swept away. She hunted down everyone she had warned of anything over the years: those people she had held back at traffic lights or told not to get on to planes, the woman whose cancer she had seen starting to seed in her belly. At first there were too few to be a pattern, but after a while it was undeniable. The woman whose cancer went into remission had seen it return full force. Her history was littered with car crashes she had stopped from happening only to have them return later. The understanding drove her mostly mad, and for six months she was sectioned, passed through different wards or halfway homes. She had never been what she thought she was. She had never been able to change anything, only ever know it was coming. She could not imagine anything worse than that.

By the time she turned up at Roger and Laura's door again she had decided to be blind in everything but the present. They did not ask where she had been or why a year had gone past without hearing from her, and she was grateful for that.

Eight years after Fiona first met Margot she woke with the worst headache she had felt for almost a decade. Why, she thought, do they call it a headache if you can feel it in your gums and your spine and your knees? She filled the sink and dropped her face into it: no good. It had been years since she'd really known anything but with the headache had come a wash of fresh, unwanted knowledge. The house muttered around her with everything that would happen. She could see the rafters caving in, the attic falling through to smother the other rooms, the water from the river rising and swallowing the garden. She did not know when it would happen, only that it would. One day the house would be gone.

As she was going back to bed she remembered what day it was. Roger's birthday. She pulled on clothes, dosed herself with the strongest painkillers she could find in the cabinet, drank vodka in the kitchen to steady herself. Helped decorate. Baked a cake that she'd known would not rise. Wore the highest shoes she had. Danced despite the nausea that swept in like a new tide underneath her, the tingling in her hands. She waited for it to come, whatever it was that was swimming towards her, slicing through possibilities until there was only one certainty left.

When she knew it she knew it simply. Margot was cutting a slice of cake. Roger and Laura were drunk, tipping in one another's arms, dancing a step no one could have named. Her eyes stretched like elastic bands in her head. She wished so hard that she didn't know, had never known anything beyond what she could see and hear and feel. She held her head in her hands and wished it gone but it was certain as iron, certain as seasons, unbendable as stone. It did not matter that she'd discovered there was no changing what would come. Perhaps, she thought, tipping forward off her chair, she'd been wrong. Perhaps this time would be different. She had to try.

When Laura and Roger went to bed Fiona found Margot in the kitchen, doing the last of the dishes. In the window Margot's face was reflected, doubling under itself, blurred.

I'm sorry, she said, and Margot looked up at her. She looked, Fiona thought, frightened already. I don't want to tell you but I know it so clearly; the way another person knows the name of the place they were born or their mother's maiden name.

Margot didn't say anything. Fiona looked at her. She wanted to take it back. She wanted a removing, a sudden seizure that swept her brain dry and arid as a desert. She would rather know nothing than know this. She took her by the shoulders and told her what she knew Margot would do. In the sink behind Margot was the washing-up bowl full of water, a scum of brownish soap. For less than an inch of time Fiona had considered bringing Margot's head down, holding it there. Drowning the happening out of her.

I don't believe you, Margot said, but they were not her words. She had always believed that Fiona could tell. I won't now I know, Margot said. Now that you've told me I'll avoid it.

You should leave now. I'll wait until you've gone, Fiona said.

She had helped Margot pack a bag of clothes, taken food from the cupboards and the fridge, filled a bottle of water at the sink. Margot sat on the bottom of the stairs, and Fiona had knelt before her and laced up her shoes. Margot had said something about leaving a message, a note, going up to say goodbye. Fiona stood at the bottom of the stairs, blocking the way, until Margot had gone.

Afterwards there was the return of years so blanched she could pick out only single objects from them: the red tag from the keys of the house she had a room in, the stub of a heel that broke off from a shoe she left somewhere, train tickets she did not remember buying or ever using. For a while she hunted those stray river doldrums in the hope that she would find Margot. Not to take her back – never that – but only to know that she was safe, that Fiona had done the right thing in sending her away. Except she never found her, never even caught a sense of her, a sniff of knowing. As if, in doing what she'd done, Fiona had shut a door she could not open again. She roamed, couldn't tell you where, mostly didn't remember. Felt herself drawn back to the cul-de-sac where Roger and Laura lived, the only place she'd ever really liked being, the curtains drawn across the windows.

The River

At first light Marcus climbed out of the tent and stood blinking, dry mouthed. The current had slowed a notch or two; the trees were standing on earth not water. There was a bite of ice. His fingers were blue. He struggled to gather kindling from the ground. When he got back, he realised he had no matches, no paper, no idea how to even make a fire. He sat in the tent wearing all his spare jumpers and with the sleeping bag around his shoulders. He thought about Sarah's arms, raised above her head, breaking out of whatever she was trapped inside. He lay back and pulled the sleeping bag over his head and thought about the way – late into the night – she'd dropped a bowl and shouted Harpiedoodle! very loudly. A word he did not think was real but that she somehow made exist just by saying it. He had never met anyone like her before. He felt as if maybe they were joined together in a way he did not understand. He wished he had never seen her; he wished he could see her every day there was left to him. Thinking, he realised this was how he'd felt when he'd seen the canal thief – that he both wanted and could not bear to see it again.

He got up. He would go to their boat and ask if she could show him how to make a fire. She would say, Of course, or, Stay here, we have a fire. He could see the shape of her mouth turning around the words, the sleeves of her T-shirt against the brown of her skin, the salty smell of her as she moved.

It was drizzling. Gretel's wind chimes turned steadily in the bushes, weighted down with the small, strung bodies. He could not see the boat for the weeds. He limped around, digging his hands into his pockets for warmth. He could hear one or the other of them singing, not words but a single note, drawn out. When he rounded the edge of the bank and saw the boat he stopped.

Sarah had connected the hose to the water tank and was holding it above herself. The ground at her feet had turned to mud. Beneath her arms there was a brush of thick, dark hair. The water fell in a stream straight onto her upturned face, mouth open. Her skin was purpling in the chill. Behind her the engine of the boat ground on.

He had seen people naked before. Walking in accidentally on Laura showering; the folds of her pink belly, the pale underside of her arms. Roger's blue-veined legs and thin bottom. Fiona through her ajar door; a stripe of buttock in between the undone zip lines, the bulge the size of a tangerine in the white underwear she wore.

This was different. It was too late not to see. The breasts – left slightly bigger – swinging as she rubbed with both hands at her hair. The press of muscle in the tops of her small arms, in the furrow of her calves. The suggestion of bone beneath – he thought of the X-ray – the edge of a hip, the scar of knee. And there, also. There also the mess of hair between her legs, black curls across her thighs. His eye drawn so immediately to it that he was not certain – when he broke away, looked up – how long she had been watching him.

When he woke later in the day Gretel was crouching over him, her nose nearly pressed to his, her hands balled on either side of his face. He held his breath. Her eyes were wide and unwavering.

I win, she said when he blinked, and she hissed a laugh. Sarah says she needs your help.

When they reached the boat a woman, the butcher, was standing smoking roll-ups on the path and spitting out stray bits of tobacco. She was tall, with tiny hands and a fuzz of hair. Next to Sarah she looked like a bear. Both of them turned to look at him as he came along and the butcher said something to Sarah that he couldn't hear but that made Sarah murmur, That's right. The butcher ducked to stub her cigarette out.

He waited for Sarah to say something about how he'd seen her, beneath the hose, but she only said, Give us a hand, gesturing to the butcher's small tug. He followed her. She touched him easily, on the hand and the shoulder, talking about something he lost track of and then could not understand. She had drawn her hair up onto her neck; it was like a rope. He marked each place she'd touched him. Here and here and here. She tutted at him, clicked her tongue. There was a scar on her neck, across the artery, as if she'd been garrotted. It only convinced him further that she was somehow invincible, somehow beyond the world that he lived in.

They went down onto the boat. The bodies were slicked in whitish lard, legs thick as his chest was wide. He couldn't tell what they were: pig or cow or sheep. The butcher's boat was as cold as a lock-up, the slabs hung from hooks set into the wall. Sarah took hold and lugged one off, heaved till he caught the base, knees bent and trembling, breath steaming out grey. Heavier than anything he'd ever carried. Coming up the riddled metal steps his bad leg went from under him and the meat pressed lovingly down onto his face while Sarah clicked her tongue somewhere above. It reminded him of carrying the body up the steps of that other boat, struggling then too. He held his breath. Felt his hands shaking.

Up, she demanded until he regained balance and stood. Come on. Mush mush.

He wanted to tell her that he had not meant to see her, to see the seam of hair or her swinging breasts, that he was sorry. Gretel was dancing on the path, tearing at the nettles as if they couldn't hurt her, kicking her feet out of her shoes, setting her hands into the mud and raising her heels over her head. There was a blue tarpaulin spread out on the ground. They laid the body down. He was starting to identify its anatomy. The jutting legs, the sliced straight edge where the head had been. There was a canvas bag of salt. Sarah showed him how to rub it into the flesh.

No, she said. Put his hand flat, placed hers over the top, pressed down. Harder, like this. Her skin was rough, thumbs like leather belt straps. They salted until he could feel the grit beneath his nails; felt as if it were he who was being preserved, his skin cured until the water couldn't get in. He thought, briefly, about what it would be like to breathe under water. It would not be so bad. No one would ever see him. He would swim. Except – he remembered – that was where the dead man was.

She took his hand again. Down, press down. He felt intensely embarrassed by how aware of every part of her he was. He tried to think of other, more logical things:

multiplications, borders between countries. She took her hand back and he felt cut, a limb missing.

It's not as thick as the last one, she said to the butcher, who was twisting them both roll-ups, Gretel pulling at her sleeve.

I dispute that. The butcher didn't look up from her hands. It's from that same farm, out by the fuel plant. They feed them straight from their own plates up there. As if they were babies.

It's thinner at the middle, Sarah said. Older. I can smell it. Lay a fair price.

He knew that Sarah would get what she wanted. The butcher's eyes were narrowed and she'd set her feet square on the ground, but Sarah was immovable as rock. He thought there had never been a time she hadn't called for something, had it given to her. He wondered what she would demand from him and felt a tug at his gut. He wondered if he should leave before that happened. He was not sure leaving was possible any more. He was anchored, wasn't he?

All right, the butcher said and put her hands in the air.

He watched as they shook, and then sat down on the edge of the bank. Gretel ferried up cups of tea, muttering and grumbling, when Sarah asked her to. He didn't say much. What would he say? When Sarah asked how it was going the butcher talked about the tidal parts of the river where the ships were big as houses and where the slip of current wrecked as many cruisers as it did at sea; about the rot that had taken the front half of her boat so that for a month she'd had to camp out in her sister's living room while it was fixed, make small talk with her sister's bad-mouthed husband.

Occasionally he looked up and saw that Sarah was eyeing him through the billows of her cigarette smoke.

Underneath his clothes he could feel that the cling film had shifted position.

Had a bit of a problem last week as well, the butcher woman said, standing up and stretching. On the roof Gretel raised herself into an unsteady handstand, tottered, fell forward.

What was that? Sarah said.

Last Monday. I didn't even hear anything but when I went out in the morning the padlock was snapped right off. Whoever it was had dragged out one of those heifers I pick up now and then from Brooke Farm, bigger than you and me put together, hacked it up on the path, taken some chunks with them.

Hacked it up?

Yup. Took some birds too. A couple of chickens. That old feller – what's his name? – only ever wants quails so I always get in a dozen or so. Lost about half of them.

Was it teenagers, do you think?

Maybe. Freaked me out. Not hearing them on the boat. I sleep light, sometimes not at all. Would have heard, I reckon, if it was kids. I normally do when they come round looking for somewhere to get drunk.

Marcus came from where you did. Heard some stuff, haven't you? Sarah said.

Yes. He swallowed, tried to look at none of them and ended up staring towards the sky, chin back.

What did you hear? the butcher woman said.

He struggled with the words. I don't know. Some fishermen said that things went missing in the night and I thought . . . I thought . . .

He had been about to tell them what he'd seen in the woods that day – silhouetted by the light – but, looking at Sarah's face, he realised how it would sound after their conversation the night before: madness, hallucinations.

Who is it then? Sarah said.

The butcher woman huffed her arms out to either side, unwilling. No idea. She knocked a clump of mud off the back of her boot. I doubt they'll come here. What would they steal? You want a couple of rabbits?

Go on then.

They watched her clambering around the side and down onto the barge, which dipped under her weight. He sat very quietly.

I can smell rain, Sarah said and got up. Need a hand? She was right; his leg had gone to sleep. The hand she held out was wide and flat like a rudder.

You can't smell rain, Gretel said.

You can. It's like iron. Let's get the lamps lit.

Gretel taught him how to play Scrabble. The fire was banked with wood and the boat was hot as an oven and lit with candles that dripped down the damp walls. He thought maybe she cheated. Words were tricky and never settled, only wriggled away like shoals of fish. He wished they could do jigsaws instead, the way he had at home, spread out across the carpet. Sometimes when he looked at the letters out of the corner of his eye he thought he might have cracked a word, but mostly he could think only of *and* or *fat* or *it*.

Nope. Gretel said. No two-letter words allowed.

That's not a rule.

Yup.

The cling film wrapped around his chest was tight and damp. He wanted to take it off, leave it in the river. Did not dare. Sarah swam in and out of the lamplight, sheathing the knife she'd used to cut the rabbit, hanging the carcasses from the roof. Moths – drawn to the light – landed on the table, opened and closed their wings. Sarah pressed forward, moved his letters around, came so close he could smell her cigarette breath on the back of his neck.

At the tent he put his hand in his pocket. Fingers touching something soft, recoiling. He took it out. The mouse's eyes caught the motion of the water and rolled like marbles. He raised his hand, thinking to throw it into the fields. Stopped himself. A thought passing over him. Bent slowly, left it at the entrance, curled, almost sleeping. Just in case it would give some sort of protection. Some sort of protection against it all: the water and the trees and the man he'd killed without meaning to and the girl with the traps and the woman, her fast hands, the dark hair that he dreamed was wrapped around his face.

The Hunt

I walked down from the house and followed the path from the bridge onto the towpath. Otto skittered ahead, ran back to check I was following, went on. The water in the canal was brown and thick. That part of the town may once have been nothing but warehouses and car parks, but it had been bought up, knocked down, developed. At the first bridge I came to skinny teenagers were lobbing themselves from the top, coming up spluttering, roaring. They sat and dried themselves on the bank with cracked cans of Stella. The sun was killer.

Now that I remembered what was there that winter it made me feel sick seeing the stones bouncing into the muck, the teenagers sucked under, their raised hands going last. A woman's pram had rolled in and she was standing on the side holding the baby and yelling for her shopping, which was starting to sink. I mistook a floating log for something it wasn't and nearly ran for the road.

I walked for two hours. It was the tail end of summer but hot enough to be the middle. There was always a fear that the seasons wouldn't come, that the solstice would rock around but the year would refuse to ebb away. There were retirees moored up, out on their deckchairs, sunning themselves, drinking red wine. A couple of them had barbeques going. At the lock a shop sold homemade cakes and ice cream; families hung over the railings to watch the gates open and close, the boats juddering through. I could smell spilt Pimm's and gin. I thought again, as I walked, about how everything ran alongside everything else; about how – if I tried hard enough – I could shout back, and my younger self would look up from the bank and hear me. I'd been spending too much time with Fiona.

I was hot and tired but I didn't want to stop where there were so many people. We walked out of the town and on until it was dark.

Otto sat chewing grass and watching me while I wrestled with the tent. It's not a pop-up, Laura had said with a degree of pride I hadn't really understood. Well she was right.

When I looked up, sweating, you were there, standing in the gloom. You had your dress hitched to your knees, which were marked with grass stains, scrapes. You were the same as you had been when I was a child. Perhaps everyone felt that way about their mothers, as if there was nothing they couldn't do. You said: *Lake Baikal is the world's deepest lake. It has more than 20 per cent of the world's unfrozen fresh water. The blue whale is the biggest animal that has ever lived. The heart of one blue whale weighs 700 kilos. An eclipse is the complete or partial obscuring of a celestial body by another.* You said, *Sleep on the roof tonight, Gretel, I need some sheesh time. I need to talk to Marcus.* You stepped closer, not leaving any mark in the weeds. Your hair had the remnants of one of my plaits in it and you looked as if you hadn't slept in weeks, your wide mouth open so that I thought, for a moment, I could smell your grassy breath. *It's here*, you said and reached out a hand towards me, the fingernails wrecked and sore-looking. I watched your mouth say the word (*Bonak*), but what came out was only a terrible static. I clamped my hands over my ears, closed my eyes. When I opened them again you were gone.

When I woke up in the morning and put the tent away I felt sick at the sound of the water slugging slowly against the banks and pulling at the trees. The ground swung beneath my feet. Otto chased ducks while I crouched with my hands on my knees. I wanted, suddenly, desperately, a cigarette because that was what you would have had. I was closer to you than ever. This was your land, your world. You never looked right anywhere else. I tried not to think about the ghost of you who'd come to visit last night, her bloody fingernails and silent mouth. There was no relief in being that close to you; I was sick with even the possibility of finding you.

I got the map out. The cities rose out of the green like mole hills, the river was an ugly blue line. We cut away from the water, across a cow field and over a stile at the other end. In the distance there was a power station: square cubes, the wires criss-crossing overhead; the noise of the water was replaced with the underground buzz of it vibrating beneath my feet.

We got lost. The tidy fields of corn and cows were gone and there were only scraps of land, dirt littered with metal barrels, half-burned sheaths of corrugated iron. An upside-down chair. I sweated dirt, spat. I was burning, marks of uneven red across my shoulders, on the bridge of my nose and the tops of my feet. Across the empty dikes and rivets there were planks of wood that gave beneath my weight; Otto didn't trust them, backing up, complaining in the bottom of his throat until I hefted him into my arms, carried him over cursing.

We came back to the river without warning. I couldn't find where we were on the map. There was a weir where the water ran slow and then plunged down. Beneath the surface there was vegetation, half rotting, half growing. In places the shore was sandy, sloping into the water. Otto went romping in, throwing up spumes of foam.

No. Bad dog.

I'd forgotten all there was to know about a river. How in some places it was so still it looked like there was a lid on the water; how the current could pick up suddenly, from the depths, churning along. We walked without much direction in mind. I looked for ways to cut off and away, but the path ran close to the bank. I stopped, spat again. There was the taste of that winter in my mouth. Otto rushed ahead, came back, rushed ahead. We still had two days of walking to go and even that was too close for comfort, I thought, and then wondered what I was doing. Why I was going there at all. I put the map away. Walked on. Slept in the tent with the door unzipped against the heat. Worried the river would infect me with watery dreams but slept through till the hot morning. Walked again. I was close. I slept and woke early. The air felt tight and the roots of the trees were bursting out through the water. Ahead the path broke open. I sped up. Reached the opening and turned away from the river The stretch of pines on my right thinned out; the wide, open space filled with overgrown grass, tufts of dandelion, swarms of thistles and nettles. A clot of bees turned in the air. There was a boat moored to the rough bank, the undergrowth edging up its sides. I got the map out, turned it this way and that. There was no doubt. It was the place we lived until I was thirteen.

The River

Days shrank and lengthened together. Two weeks went past. His parents came back to him. He thought, I miss you, I love you, I want you to find me, I'm sorry. He thought about the day spent on the boat with Charlie's body. He remembered what he'd hidden beneath his clothes and it seemed too big a secret for just one person to have. It was so cold there was frost hardening the side of his tent, the edge of the river, in silver lines from the trees. In the mornings he was so lonely he could barely see.

But in the quick afternoons and the slow evenings it was different. Sarah showed him how to find wild garlic, buried deep. In the summer, she said, there were mushrooms in the ground and apples on some of the trees. She showed him how to knead bread and filter homebrew so it was the colour of amber.

He began to understand more of the words they used though he didn't feel brave enough to speak them himself. Sarah called Gretel El or sometimes Hansel or Regretel. Gretel called Sarah Dudey or Doctor. To have sheesh time meant that Sarah needed some time alone. A harpiedoodle was a small annoyance like a dropped plate or scratch but was used often, mostly shouted, to denote anything that hadn't gone quite to plan. Something comfortable or enjoyable, often soft or warm, was duvduv – named after a blanket Gretel had as a child and then lost. There were more words for the sound the water made or the river in different seasons and temperature than he could remember. He understood that effie meant the current was faster as in the water was effing along or effying along the banks; that sills was the noise the river made at night and grear the taste of it in the morning. Often they used a word he did not know and he would see Sarah looking at him and wonder if, somehow, she liked that he did not always understand, that there were still secrets he was not included in. The more he listened the more he understood that the words were instinctual, formed from the sounds things made or words Gretel had come up with as a baby which had stuck. Watching them he realised that it had been just them for so long it did not matter if no one understood. They had cut themselves off from the world linguistically as well as physically. They were a species all their own. He wanted to be like them, he wanted to be them.

When he wasn't with Sarah he followed Gretel as she emptied her traps and refilled the wind chimes with the dead bodies of mice and frogs. She read him every book there was on the boat. Her favourite was the battered encyclopedia, with its dense, ant-sized writing and bright photos. In the mornings she had lessons with Sarah which consisted – as far as he could see – of reading this book. She knew a lot of the entries off by heart. Anastasia was a Russian princess who died and for years people pretended to be her. The Styx is one of the rivers of the underworld. She wouldn't let him touch, but she held it open and turned the pages so he could see. She liked the water creatures best. He wondered if she liked them because they were easier to imagine there than the lions or elephants. They could be in the river and no one would know, going carefully through their lives: the horned whales, sharks, turtles, trout and salmon. She liked the pictures of the ocean, the measurements of its depths, the illustrations of how rivers were formed, cutting through stone. She liked bullet-point facts which she'd snap out at him. Did you know that a naked mole rat is the longest living rodent? That they have colonies and queens the way bees do?

I don't know anything about that, he said. He liked it when she spoke about stars, the smears of luminous gas joined to one another with their own secret, internal locking of gravity. They came in pairs or clusters, rarely alone. There was something about space, the bulges of busy planets and stars, each orbiting one another, the logic of gravitational fields, the stars dying long before we got to see them.

He had got distracted and Gretel was annoyed that he wasn't listening.

Look at this, she said. The animal in the picture had a thick scab of skin across its back and sides and a soft creamy belly.

It can live for a hundred years. She widened her eyes at him. You can tell how old it is by the rings on its bones. It can see in the dark. It can hear and smell very well.

OK.

She pressed her face towards the page.

What's it called? he asked but she would not tell him.

It's a riddle, she said or he thought she did.

What do you mean?

But she was already up and off the boat, running.

Sarah and Gretel called anything that came by in the river (fish, planks of wood, plastic bags) a sprung. People on boats were human-sprungs; carcasses or sheep or waterlogged birds were dead-sprungs. He waited for the river to bring his parents to him but all it brought were junkers piled with bicycles and bags of coal; barges strung with dirty flags and broken windows. The boats moored up alongside for an hour or so. All of the people passing knew Sarah by name, looked at him curiously, tried to grab and hug Gretel. They drank tea or brought out crates of beer which Sarah broke open on the side of the boat. They looked sleep-worn, the skin stretched too tight across their arms and faces, the marks of their nails on the insides of their hands. When Sarah asked where they were going they told her away from there. South, a man said, as far south as we can go. They spoke about noises in the dark, marks on the muddy banks, something heavy on the roofs of their boats. When she asked them to stay a night they would not, told them they should come too. Hauled off from the shore, drove on, not looking back.

There was a cold snap. The tent poles broke; the edge of the river hardened to ice, birds fell from the trees to the solid ground. A final boat came. A man and woman with three children, whom Gretel gathered together like a herd and spirited down below. They had nervous, twisting hands and were grey, the colour turned down across their faces. They spoke almost too quietly to hear. Sarah brought out homebrew and filled mugs. The woman was drunk already or sick. Her words slopped over one another or did not come out at all. They spoke about a fourth child, a boy, whom they no longer had. Marcus sat silently; his hands felt too big for his wrists. Their grief was bare, like a strong light. Sarah asked why they had left, what if the boy came back and they were not there? He heard only every other word they said and could not make sense of half of those. They left with the things Sarah had given them: a chicken, a couple of bottles of homebrew, some blankets.

I don't understand, he said.

Sarah was gathering together the mugs. There was nobody to wait for, she said, there was a body. She cleared her throat into her balled fist. Fucking cigarettes. She dropped the mugs into the bucket of washing-up water.

When Gretel was a child, she said, she wouldn't talk about death so we called it leaving and sometimes she'd ask if things were coming back, when would they come back. Even now I think sometimes she waits for a dog we had years ago or a couple of friends who've died. She told me she didn't think they would come back the same. She wouldn't explain what that meant only that when the leaving was done they'd return different.

He didn't know what to say. He was still not used to the way she sometimes spoke without pause or need for collusion.

I know your tent is shot to shit. You can sleep here tonight if you'd like to.

He was relieved. He knew that, in the night, the tent would fill with everything he'd heard: the small body of that boy and of Charlie, the bottom of his sleeping bag opening out to the river, the dead coming back with other people's voices or thoughts. She made more tea and they sat on the steps drinking it. There were the quiet noises of Gretel asleep. He could feel Sarah's arm against his. He thought about the fourth child.

Why didn't they call someone? he said.

Who would they call?

The police?

No. They wouldn't have done that.

He did not understand. He sat quietly.

What would they have said to the police? she said after a moment. Would they have told them about the things they'd seen – the things everyone else had seen – in the water? How they knew what had taken their child although they couldn't explain what it was.

Maybe.

And then when the police said, That's not possible; things like that don't happen here. Tell us what really happened to your child. What would they say?

I don't know.

They would say, We saw it. We know what it was. You need to catch it. And the police would say, You're lying to us. What are you trying to hide? Do you understand?

Maybe, he said.

She shook her hands out as if drying them of water. We don't call the police here. We don't call the fire engines or the ambulances. It's always been that way. They don't know anything about us and we know all we need to about them.

But what happens when something goes wrong?

We look after it, she replied and stood with a finality that told him there was no more to be said.

That was the first night he slept on the boat but it was not the last. He pulled the hood of his sleeping bag over his head and filled it with his breath. The fire burned until morning. Gretel talked in her sleep as if, even then, she could not contain the words. Sarah slept so quietly he wondered if she slept at all. He could feel her not far away, lying on her back. Her presence was sharp, startling.

In the night the river rushed from the north, brought the silver bellies of fish twisting in the slurry, the decking of a boat broken up by the current, twists of autumn leaves from places where the seasons had dragged and winter only just come, sprays of salt and pebbles from the sea. There were more Bonak in the water than could be counted: bodies whose ghosts might catch on the anchor and decide to stay, trunks of trees big enough to sweep the boat away, the canal thief who rose out of the rip-tide tunnels and hesitated.

Six

Formed of Debris

The River

A late, cold-dazed bee had stung him and Sarah was sucking out the barb. He looked down at her parting, chalked in the dark hair. Her bare feet jiggled on the floor, one hand clamped around his arm to hold him still. What am I doing here? he thought and then she straightened with the sting clamped between her teeth like a needle.

Do you want to keep it?

She laid it flat on his hand. It's good luck. Especially so late in the season. They die when they sting you. I thought we could cook up a storm tonight. What do you think? A feast. A no-holds-barred banquet.

Yes, he said.

She pressed the side of her face against his cheek. She seemed young that morning, exuberant or nervous. Earlier – out in the scrub – he'd watched her and Gretel doing handstands, tipping their ankles above their heads. Gretel's legs wavered, dipped, but Sarah's were very straight and still. He'd felt a sharp pain on his wrist, and when he looked the bee was hunched over, stippled back dropped towards the skin.

*

Sarah flung open the doors of the boat and cleaned on hands and knees, throwing buckets of dirty water out into the river. He bent beside her to help. She was sweating. He wanted to ask if she was worried by all that they'd heard but he did not. He knew there were things they were not talking about: the dead boy, the butcher woman's broken-into boat, everyone fleeing except for them. Some of the passing boats had left them meat, fresh bread, a slab of very yellow butter. They would have a feast, a banquet.

You could do with a wash, she said sniffing and then laughing. When did you last have one? Take my towel. There's some washing-up liquid in that bucket. That smell you've got is what Gretel used to call a good one when she was little and hated washing. As in I've got a good one.

He lifted an arm, pressed his face into the crease of armpit. It was true: he had never smelled so bad. It had been nearly a month since the last time he'd washed – in the narrow shower at his parents' house – worn clean clothes, seen his own body. His hair was crustacean-like.

Be careful, Sarah said. The current's strong this time of year. It'll wash you away.

He hesitated. He wanted to tell her that he was too afraid; he could not go into the water. The canal thief was there, somewhere near the bottom, waiting.

Don't worry, she said. That uncanny way she had of seeming to know what he was thinking. She pulled him towards her for a moment, her arms around his shoulders. Don't worry. If you go that way there's a sheltered bit among the trees. I'll be able to hear if you call for me.

He felt momentarily enraged. The way she talked to him as if he were a child like Gretel; the way she presumed he would shout for her. A moment later he was not angry any longer. She would come if he called. She knew what he was thinking.

He stopped at the tent, took the roll of cling film and some underwear that he could scrub near clean, leave to dry.

At the corner before the weir the river widened and – off to one side – there was a thin sliver of water, inaccessible by boat from the river – the entrance overcrowded with stripped trees – but easy to get to from the land. He hesitated on the bank above. He'd been so careful, keeping his distance from the river, making sure he never – if he could help it – turned his back on it or forgot it was there. Most days he made sure to remind himself of what he'd seen that time underneath the trees; of what all those people were afraid of. He could go back, say nothing, try and wash from a bucket, hide some of the smell. He raised his armpit again, sniffed, turned his head and smelled his hair, which had started to grow back, tufts around his ears. It was true. It was a good one. It hurt his gums to think of her smelling him like that, knowing how dirty he was. She was cooking dinner, she wanted him to come and eat with them, he'd been sleeping on their boat for nearly a week. He would do whatever she asked him to. If she asked him to go under the water and never come back he would. He told himself that it was a debt of gratitude for all she'd done but he already knew it was more than that.

He skidded down the bank and landed on his backside in the water. It was very cold. Never mind. He skimmed aside the layer of algae. Struggled his arms out of the first T-shirt, pulled the rest off in a clump, daring himself.

Fumbled out of the trousers and dunked them straight into the mire, whirling to try and get rid of the stench. Pants went the same way. He'd been wearing the cling film for so long it had moulded against his body, held on when he tried to prise it loose. Then it was gone. He dropped awkwardly to his knees, threw the water in handfuls over his shoulders and back. Squirted a glob of washing-up liquid and lathered it up, rubbing hard and then rinsing.

Odd to see it again. The breasts were bigger than they had been, bottle-nosed, fleshy. The rest was thinner, the folded belly sucked around the too-big ribcage. His hands were shored with tight red bumps from the nettles by the boat, legs patterned with bruises. There was a rough scaling of dirt – almost reptilian – which he scrubbed at. The hair between his legs was thicker, knotted. He caught himself pressing a hand through it, searching for what wasn't there, what hadn't grown just from him thinking of it. His body reminded him of something. He cupped a breast, held it, felt a twanging go from toes to top. Knew then that he was reminded of Sarah underneath the stream of water, both arms raised. He sat down, skidded a little further down the bank so that he could feel the current passing across his feet. He watched his skin coming out from under the grime. Braced his feet on the roots that grew out from the mud and leaned forward to lift handfuls to his face. Slipped and was under the water before he knew what was happening. He opened his eyes in the dim. Could just about make out the pale, ghostly shape of his feet out in front of him. Remembered – the electricity of it shooting through him – the way he had tipped the dead man in. Tipped him into the water. Trying to pull himself backwards, mouth open and gabbling for air. How the dead man (*Charlie Charlie Charlie*) had sunk, and how he'd thought that all the rivers were connected and everything now was connected to that body, dropping below the surface.

He came out, retching for air.

The Hunt

There was a chain around the boat's door handles and – when I pressed my face against the window – the glass was too dirty to see through. On the scrub there was an overturned wheelbarrow with sticky weed growing through its wheel loops, some noodle pots. The grass looked as if it had been burned a couple of times, grown back sickly. There was also a blue Volvo. The door opened when I tried it. The seats were mouldering and there was the imprint of hands in the steering wheel. In the glove box there was a map of Scotland, a couple of dried-out packets of tobacco. In the back there was a mess of crisp bags, clouded water bottles, empty egg and cheese sandwich containers. I could feel my hands shaking as I picked things up. Was it your car? I straightened, looked around, shouted your name. Was it yours or just someone's abandoned cruiser, left to rot? I wanted it so badly to have belonged to you. This first physical sign of you, living, walking, leaning out the window. I imagined you driving fast, past Manchester and the Lakes, knocking the chair back to sleep. What were you looking for? Not stopping to eat, the rubbish thrown into the footwell. Singing along to the radio. Thinking of me as I was thinking of you. Maybe

Marcus was in the seat next to you. Maybe you spoke about me together, said you would come back soon, you wanted to see me soon.

I scouted around the field beyond. Otto was pressing here and there with his nose, huffing and looking back at me as if impatient to be gone. This was where I'd been heading. This was, probably, where I should have come right at the start. The places we were born came back to us. Still, it did not feel right to be there. Above the thick pines there were birds that wheeled and gathered. I remembered thinking about dread back at the cottage, right at the start of all this. There was dread here too. What would be found; what might never be found; what I was too late to find. The river seemed barely to move and, near the banks, was shallow enough to see the rocks. Leaning over to look set a rolling in my stomach, and when I pitched back the sky seemed to upend itself. I caught the ground with my knees, put my cheek against the grass. When I turned to look for Otto he wasn't there. I stood shouting for him, but if anything came across the field towards me I did not see it.

I wanted, suddenly, to be done with it. To be done with it all. I did not want to be there looking at a car that might or might not be yours. I wanted it over. I found a bottle of petrol on the boat and emptied it out onto the damp seats of the Volvo, wiped my hands on the grass. It didn't go up as fast as I'd imagined but tindered for a good while and then suddenly took. There were trees not as far away as they should be and I imagined I might burn the whole forest down. It would not matter. There was nothing here. I should have known. The car burned so hot I retreated, stood on the roof of the boat to watch it.

The lock on the door was harder to break than I thought it would be. I scouted around for something I could use to force it open. I was unhappy with the thought of being aboard but more afraid of staying outside. At the far end of the boat, under a green tarpaulin, I found a spade. The handle was damp but it would do the job. I jammed it against the padlock and heaved.

The steps down into the boat had rotted and my foot went straight through. For a sickening moment I thought that it was the boat we had lived on for all that time, but it was different: there were dirty porthole windows, shelves hammered onto the curving walls, a pile of blankets. A clinging heat. The stove had long been ripped out; the chimney opened onto the sky. There was nothing else. Something skittered at the far end. I went noisily, clomping my boots in case of snakes. Everything smelled musty, left too long. The blankets fell apart as I lifted them. I had forgotten what it was like to have every step repeated by an answering movement from the boat; the water under your feet. I settled beneath the pillar of chimney light. Ate some of the bread I'd brought from the house.

I must have fallen asleep at some point because I woke sweating, went out to piss. The body of the car was still smoking, and there were holes in the hard dirt around it. I kicked at them with my boots. Not moles or rabbits but symmetrical, straight sided; done with the spade, which I found not far away, stuck into the ground. They seemed significant, like pre-language signs that I did not understand. I had heard nothing, and it set my teeth thinking of someone foraging around without my knowing. I retreated to the boat, put my sleeping bag on the roof and sat on it. Mostly there were only birds, which took off from the pines, a couple of squirrels, the sound of the water. It was warm the way I never remembered it being and I caught myself dozing, the white imprint of heat on my eyelids, feet braced against the runnel so I didn't roll.

When I came to properly there was someone thumping around in the boat beneath me. I hefted the spade in one hand, practised swinging it through the air. Stepped down onto the aft of the boat and kicked the door to one side. I could hear the whistle of its breath, the shift of its weight on the sodden floor. When I moved further in it was so dark I could make out only the side of its body, upright, long-armed, the white dome of its head. The Bonak. Come back. What we were afraid of all along. I lifted the spade up above my shoulder.

You stepped forward out of the dim and peered at me, one hand shading your face from the shaft of light. I dropped the spade and it rebounded, nearly hit me in the face. I put my arms out towards you and you looked at me suspiciously.

Why did you burn my car? you said.

I reached for you, tried to touch your face and hair, your arms. You hissed, batted me away. You wouldn't believe me when I told you who I was.

Gretel, you kept saying, was shorter and her hair was not that colour. Why did you burn my car?

You seemed flighty, nervous. I kept my distance and you kept yours. It seemed impossible that you were there, that I had found you. I kept waiting for you to break, make for the trees. If you did – I told myself – I would chase you. I felt frantic, a little hysterical; you were there, fleshy, toothy, whole. I wanted to tie you to me to stop you from leaving again. You moved carefully around me as if afraid I might lunge for you. I wanted to lunge for you. I wanted to wrap my arms around you and not let go. I'd never been an adult with you before. I could feel myself reverting, sliding back. I wanted you to cook for me, sing me to sleep, wash my hair and then plait it. You were my mother. I was thirteen years old again; I was sixteen. You brought me dried-out pastries from Greggs, you cried in the night, we fought. I was not angry; I loved you.

Do you have any food? you asked.

No.

You did not look at me straight on. I positioned myself under the light from the hole in the ceiling hoping you would recognise me. I wanted so badly for your face to suddenly clear in realisation, for you to say that you'd been looking for me for years and that everything would be fine now that you had found me. I wanted you to tell me that there were explanations for everything that had happened: for you leaving in the first place, for you being the sort of mother you were. I felt a sudden, shocking heat that said I might weep openly and desperately in front of you. I couldn't remember the last time I cried. I pinched the sides of my nose hard enough for the feeling to go away.

El was younger, you said obstinately, planting your hands on your hips in a move I remembered; marking an end to the conversation.

I studied you, tried to take in the whole of you at once. You had aged too. I could see your body sagging under your clothes, loose around the belly. Your face had some new give to it, the cheeks a little puffy, a wattle along your neckline. You had shrunk, were even shorter than I remembered. There was, though, muscle still in your arms and in the calves of your legs, which I saw when you hitched at your trousers, scratched at the skin. Your fingers were yellowing and I waited for you to light up the way you always did. But you only occasionally patted at your hip pocket and then clicked in a way so like you I found myself searching over your shoulder, looking for my young mother, who would click or hum or whistle in annoyance or mirth or impatience. At your chest the T-shirt bulged on one side and then, on the other, hung loosely. I stared. Tried to look away. Could not. Kept staring. You looked at me, peering as if you couldn't see quite as well as you used to.

Do you have any food?

No.

What are you doing on my boat?

There was no one here, I said.

You seemed interested by this, holding your face in your hands. I thought that I was here, you said.

When it started getting dark you began to shake with the cold. The feeling of needing to grab at you had not gone away; I restrained myself from wrapping you up in the sleeping bag, pulling you to the floor, pressing my face against you. You were my mother. You were my mother.

I wanted to find wood to make a fire but was afraid that, if I turned my back, you would leave again.

Shall we go outside? I said and you followed me but wouldn't come close. I listened to you calling curses up at the pines, snapping branches between your wide hands. When I started making the fire you nudged me aside, muttering at the bad job, rebuilt the pyramid I had started ineptly making.

The flames lighting upwards did something to your face and body, spinning time, and it was like sitting across from you the way you were then. Looking at you I could feel something in me beginning to cave in, give way. A resolution or determination; an adultness. I had thought there would be anger but mostly there was relief. I had found you. After all this time. You were there. I opened my mouth to try and explain, tell you, and you glared at me across the fire.

What are you doing on my boat? you said. Who are you? What do you want? Why did you burn my car? I was going to drive it.

I don't know who burned it. I didn't even know you could drive.

When I said things like that you went quiet, poked at the flames with the toe of your boot or sang a couple of lines of a tune I did not remember or recognise. Your hair had gone white from top to bottom and was longer than I had ever seen it. You pulled up the sleeves of your coat and trousers and bared your legs to the fire. There were scars you did not have when I knew you. A nasty one on your calf that I pointed at.

How did you get that?

You shrugged, prodded it with your finger. An accident.

You laughed, laughed until you coughed. Have you met Gretel? You held your arms against your chest as if rocking a child, looked around. She must be sleeping.

I haven't, I said. Do you live here with Gretel?

You nodded, nudged at the fire with your boot. I left my first baby. You looked at me carefully through the flames. So now it's just Gretel. Do you remember, you said, the first boat? Do you remember the baby?

No.

Your hands were clenched against your chest, your mouth quavering. I felt almost ashamed to see you that way. Your younger self had no time for weakness or hesitation. I reached out towards you again and you jerked back, yowling, your feet scrabbling at the dirt.

I phoned her. I asked her to come. But she hasn't yet.

It's me, Sarah. I got your message and the email. I've been looking for you.

You blew air into your cheeks so they bulged. I'm clumsy, you said. I lose things so easily. The other day I lost the car keys and now I'm stuck here. Maybe we could find them together. There are other things. Other things I lost. We could find them all.

Maybe, I said.

We could find the baby.

I'm here, Mum. I'm not a baby any more.

You leaned forward over the fire and took me by the side of the head so fast you blurred, your fingernails were long and I felt the blood from my cheek. Feeling your hands on my face blew the air right out of me. For god's sake, Gretel, you said. For god's sake.

The River

The feast. They ate salted pork with their fingers. There were potatoes cooked in cream and bread with cheese. The fire rose up the chimney. Sarah refilled his glass so often he lost count, the numbers turning in his head like wind dials. It was sweet, unsettled his belly. He ate more pork, breaking the crackling between his teeth. He ate until he was full and then, when she filled his plate again, ate more. He dipped in and out of the conversation. Gretel was dozing, her face in the crook of her arms, her mouth open as she breathed.

Sarah sat back against the wall, pushed her legs out in front of her. He looked at her mouth and the white of her neck between dress and shoulders. He came around on hands and knees and – before he could think not to do it – put his head into her lap. He could feel the wine booming a second pulse in his wrists, between his fingers. She had her hands on his head, in the folds of hair, against his temples, which ached.

I went under the water, he said. When I was washing I went under the water.

He could feel the words bubbling out of him, out of control. Her hand kept moving over his head, pressing the hair down.

It's OK, she said before he could tell her what he'd done. That he'd killed a man. That he'd killed a man and dropped him into the river. She pushed him up off her lap with one hand, stood, knocked a glass empty against her mouth. There was a bucket of water she'd boiled earlier, filled with suds. She took the plates off the table one by one and pushed them in. He could see how hot the water was by the red lines on her arms, the steam that dampened her face and wet her hair. She turned, wrapping her hands in the front of her dress to dry them.

Do you ever think, she said, what it might look like?

He was drunk enough that for a moment the question did not make sense. He focused on her. Yes, I do, he said. Although he was uncertain if this was true. If he had ever really considered the possibility of the Bonak looking like anything.

I do too, she said. She sounded young, Gretel-like, her hands still balled in the folds of her dress. I've been thinking about it recently. I know Gretel has as well.

She did not ask him what he thought it looked like. She told him that when she imagined the Bonak it had a long body, strong-muscled legs, a pale belly, a jagged mouth with teeth that hung over the soft edge. It could swim fast in the water, of course, but it could also move fast on the land. It could digest anything it ate. It could eat anything it chose. It was clever. It could learn human language if it wanted, although – she suspected – it did not want to. Why would it?

He went and dried while she washed. Gretel made quiet sleeping noises behind them. He could feel the heat from her shoulder next to him.

I think maybe you should leave in the morning, she said. I don't know where you came from but you should go back there.

I can't go back, he said.

Well you can go somewhere other than here. It's not good you being here. It's not right. Find a town. A train station. Some place that doesn't even know somewhere like this exists. There are lots of places like that. Everybody forgets. You will too. Anything can be lost if you try hard enough.

She picked up the bottle and tilted it towards her mouth so that he could see her sharp teeth through the glass. Before you go, though, I need your help with something. Will you help me?

Yes. Of course. OK.

The lump, she said, was in her armpit, near the bottom. She had felt it a week before but it was nearly impossible to tell without help. You felt, she said, what you imagined rather than what was really there. They could hear Gretel sleeping, breathing loudly through her nose, her feet jerking like a dog having a rabbit chasing dream.

What do you want me to do?

She showed him how to splay his hands, the fingers interlaced, how to knead down.

You are looking for something that does not belong, that should not be there.

The bone in his leg felt like it had been struck, began to vibrate. There were blue veins like map contours on her breast and, around the nipple, a smattering of dark hair. She showed him the point, below her armpit. He pressed forward with his hands.

Harder.

Kneaded down into the soft flesh. Her breast was wedged against his shoulder and he could smell her breath. It was too much, then, to stand.

No, he said. I don't feel it. Though, just as he pulled away, he thought maybe he did. A small bite of gristle.

That's good, she said and pulled the top down. Just let me know if you want me to check for you. Before you go.

What? He ducked his head away from her.

Anytime. I'll check. Sleep now.

The Hunt

I stayed with you on the river, sleeping on the boat, building fires to chase away the night cold, eating food straight from the tins in my bag. I got used to being with you; stopped worrying that I would wake and find you gone. You seemed to get used to me too. One morning you called me Gretel in an offhand way as if you'd never doubted it. You clucked at me, stroked your hands against my cheek, tried to brush the knots out of my hair. What are you doing here? How did you find me? You spat onto your hand and rubbed at dirt on my face. When I went to fetch more logs for the fire you always trailed me, catching at my hands or pulling, a little hard, at my hair.

It's duvduv to see you, Gretel, you said. At that ancient word I felt my stomach dropping away. You said it with a curl, a lift, which is not the way I thought it was said. It's so duvduv. I closed my eyes.

At other times you were so lost that I let you be. You drew in the dirt or hunched down and looked into the fire. You crouched and pushed your pants down, pissed where you'd been sitting. I wanted to tell you everything that had happened to me but you were a sieve and anything you retained was peppered with holes or formed of debris.

At first light on the third day that I'd been there you clawed your way onto the roof of the boat and pointed over the trees.

He sleeps in the day, you shouted.

I climbed up after you. You lay down on your back and I lay next to you. You pointed out constellations in the sky to me though it was daytime. You grasped my hand and held it, your nails digging into my palm.

Who does? Who sleeps in the day?

You didn't answer me. There were the final shadings of a moon, already fading. The heat was coiled beneath the weight of the morning. The river was effing along, heavy with sprung. I slept, a little, and when I woke up you were gone. There was heat wave across the scrub, the stink of hot earth. This was bastard land, the mess of railways beyond the trees, the rotting lock. There was a thin sheet of dust over everything, as if from a volcano or storm. I looked for you on the boat but you were not there and you were nowhere in the scrub or by the water. I trekked through the forest feeling pissed off and shouting for you. This place sucked people away, swallowed them whole. I'd even lost the dog.

There was a movement through the trees, bodily, flickering. You were halfway down the bank with your arms submerged nearly to the shoulders and your dress sodden around your haunches. I said your name and you twisted to look back at me. You smiled craggily around your wide teeth.

You just missed him, you said, he was here a moment ago.

Except when I looked out at the water I thought maybe I did see it for a second, just beneath the surface, gone.

*

I understood then that when you sent me the email you had not found Marcus as I'd hoped; you'd found the Bonak instead. When I knew what I was looking for it was obvious what was here. There were signs everywhere, tracking all around the boat, in the trees, across the dirt. It had been in all the places we had. You showed me the telltale marks: the banks rubbed smooth or scored with claw lines; the underwater pantry beneath the raised roots of a water-bound tree where we could just make out a sheep. The grass was flattened beneath its weight. Even the top of the boat was marked with its distinctive five clawed lines.

It sleeps, you told me, with its mouth open and sometimes with one eye too.

You seemed serene, calm, even contented. I thought of the way you'd crouched in the water, reaching out. There had been something almost companionable about it. As if you'd grown old and so had it. As if you'd come to an agreement.

But you killed it, I said to you again and again. You ignored me. I thought, I said, that you killed it? You lifted your dress up over your knees, shook your arms. You smiled at me, a beautiful, peaceful smile. I remembered you telling me that you killed it. That night at the end of the long winter.

I watched the memory solidifying in front of me. I remembered how you'd fixed the lamp to the front of the boat and set me there to watch for debris, tree trunks so big they'd capsize the boat. You'd drawn a blanket around my shoulders, pressed an icy kiss onto my forehead. Where's Marcus? I'd said and your face had seemed insubstantial in the dim, your eyes closing for longer than a blink.

He'll follow us soon.

Is the Bonak dead? I asked.

Yes, you said. Not hesitating. I killed it last night.

It had never even crossed my mind that you might have lied.

All the years I had been searching for you, you'd been hunting for the Bonak. You spoke of it in almost religious terms; it was a crusade. You believed, I thought, that it was a sort of penance. A pound of flesh. You spoke proudly of it – your quest – but to me it seemed like a recurring nightmare one of us might have had.

After you left me at the stables you'd gone back to the river, but it was long gone by then. You told me about picking up the signs, listening out. A cat killer somewhere near the flight of Birmingham locks. A whole field of sheep gone in a single night. The clothes of some children who'd been walking home found in the river. You trekked boatyards, canal communities, places the police wouldn't go because they didn't even know they were there. Boat people liked a good story. You climbed the country like a ladder and Scotland opened to receive you.

Years of dead ends, lost trails and then finally, in a small Highland river, you'd seen it again. It seemed slower moving than you remembered, almost tired as it slid down a bank and out of sight. You were older too, less certain. By the time you'd plunged knife first into the water it was gone.

You followed it from south to north and back again. The Bonak – as if knowing who was on its tail – had swum until it reached the place by the pines and then stopped. You saw it clambering up onto land, basking in the sun, digging itself into the sodden mud to cool. You watched it chasing the docile, lazy fish or lying in wait for rodents who came to the water to drink. It was clever. You watched it hanging beneath the surface with sticks in its mouth and catching the birds that came to collect them for their nests. There was a sort of coexistence. You sometimes sat out on the roof of the old boat you'd found there and sang with the creature in the water beneath you, listening. You sometimes caught rabbits in your traps and ate only half, throwing the rest to it. You told me this in fragments, as we looked for wood or listened to the water passing. You were, while you talked, like before, nothing had changed, you knew everything that had gone by. I watched these moments of lucidity with dread, knowing they wouldn't last long. You told me, and cried, how you'd forgotten why you'd been following it, what the point of it all had been. You forgot entirely that you'd meant, all along, to kill it.

The River

They fished for chub or pike. Sarah was brooding at the opposite end of the boat, legs hung down, the end of the rod pressed against her belly as she drew the line out, threw it further than either he or Gretel could.

In the morning when he woke Sarah had packed his bag and left it at the foot of the mattress. He'd moved around her in narrowing circles of anxiety, waiting for her to tell him he had to go. His hands remembered the feel of the night, the nodule he thought that maybe he had felt beneath her armpit. He couldn't be sure. She scrubbed at plates caked with food, cut a wizened apple into chunks and bullied Gretel into eating it. She said little to him, only asked if he'd ever fished before. Once, he said. She showed him how to press the worm down onto the hook. He understood that it was his choice to go and that she would not tell him to. He understood – also – that he couldn't leave. More than that: he couldn't ever leave her.

There was in his rod a tensing, then a juddering. His hands were damp and slipped over the mechanism, fumbled, almost dropped it. The line went down trembling. Just beneath it he could see the snicker of movement. The tip of the fish came out. It was heavy-headed, the hook pushed through its fat lip, grey body snaking behind. Gretel had come up beside him and was watching, bent on all fours.

Get it. Get it in, she said.

He looked for Sarah, wanting her to see. For a moment the water seemed to suck the fish back down. Then the tail came out, forked. He wedged his feet against the narrow bar, rocked the balance off his bad leg. The fish thrashed itself sideways in the air, as long as his arm, eyes the colour of the buttons on the front of Gretel's coat, which she had shrugged off, held out to wrap it in. He drew it towards the boat.

The Bonak came straight up underneath, jaws cracked to either side. Its rocky back was the colour of moss, its belly soft and pale, short muscled legs curving downwards, pushing up. Its body moving in such a way that suggested it was not made of what the rest of them were, was boneless, composed only of flesh. It looked – he had the time to think – just the way Sarah had described it. The fish was for a moment framed between the rise of its teeth and then was gone. He felt the awful pull on the rod, his feet skidding out from beneath him, falling onto the side of his bad leg. Then the line was broken, the rod dropping from his hands and into the water.

Seven

The Bonak

The River

I think we need to catch it, Sarah said. The Bonak. We're going to catch it.

He hoped that she would change her mind and they would unmoor and ride down the river and away. She would forget she had ever told him to leave and he would come on the boat with them, live with them forever.

We need – as if she could hear his doubting – to catch it.

On the table Gretel put out one of her old rodent catchers and took it apart so they could see how it worked. Sarah hummed with approval at the intelligence of it, the strength of the jaws, the coiled mechanism. She had been fidgety all night, not sitting still, rising and moving things around, clicking her fingers or shuffling her feet against the floor. At one point she had stood over him, looking down, her fat lip pressed between her white teeth, her arms crossed over and her hands tapping at her hips.

What? he'd said.

Nothing.

But still she had stared at him with her eyes drawn nearly closed. He did not know what she wanted. He felt his face grow hot and he looked away, busied himself with other things, felt her gaze on the back of his neck.

Gretel showed them how to create the tension, how to lever the weight down so it rested lightly, would snap at a moment's pressure. There would be a cage, baited at one end, with a door that lowered. There was not enough room in the boat so they carried everything they needed out onto the bank and worked on it there. The sides of the cage were pieces of old fence from the scrub wound together with wire, the weights were old diesel cans filled with stones. Sarah took off the door of the boat and attached it to one end of the cage. The trap was just big enough to take a person lying down if they bent their knees, but a person standing would be uncomfortable.

We could go into the forest, find the nearest town, he said loudly. They both looked at him. We could just go, he said.

Further down the river, past us, there are more boats, whole families aboard, she said and then fell silent. He understood that what she was saying was that if they didn't catch it more people would die. He thought of the fourth child. His skin was wrinkled from so many nights in the water, his eyes were white. He thought that going back to his parents – after everything that had happened – would be the same: as if he'd died and come back changed, a different person entirely.

The trap was clunky, ungainly. The cans swung against the front and made a racket. It was heavy, difficult to move.

It doesn't need to hold for very long. Sarah said. It's not a war; it's a small battle. By the end of the week everything will be back to normal.

He did not understand what she meant. Nothing would ever be the same again. She brought out the final leftovers from the pig carcass, shunted them to the end of the trap. Covered the wire with a scattering of dead leaves, a couple of branches.

It's a lure, he said, remembering.

Sarah looked at him. How do you know about those?

He did not answer. She shook her head.

Next to him Gretel did not chitter or dance but hung still from the edge of the boat, watching. He wondered, looking at her, if she had known all along what it was. The pages in the encyclopedia she had shown him, her empty traps, all her talk of riddles. He tried to remember what it had looked like as it came out of the water, curved, and took the fish from his line. Already the memory was fading, and he was uncertain what parts of it he remembered badly or filled in wrong.

Where shall we go when this is over? Sarah said and swung Gretel's hand, smiled at him. What country shall we go to?

I don't know.

Somewhere hot. You'd look better with a tan.

Yes, he said and meant it with everything he had. Yes.

Sarah had decided they would anchor the boat in the middle of the river so they were as far from the trap as they could get and still keep watch. They checked the mooring and then loosed the boat and let it swing out into the current, the ropes falling into the water and then pulling, tensed, to the bank. He dropped the anchor; couldn't see it a second after it was gone, jolting down towards the bottom. The river was very high and fast. He clutched the tiller. On the roof

Gretel was crouched, gripping on. The current thudded into the side of the boat. On the bank the trap seemed watchful, wholly aware. Above their heads something flew past, a bat perhaps, bending its arrowed wings.

When Marcus woke in the night there was a wet heat. Brackish moisture around the corners of the boat, the smell of sprouting garlic rising from the walls. He could feel the last threads of the dream he'd been having tangling about his face. There had been the sitting room of his parents' house, the curtain rails hung with lights, the remains of cake on the wooden table, the sink filled with soapy water. He could hear movement upstairs and from the river outside, which sounded as if it was battering the walls of the garden, rising up the bridge. As it had been it was again. Fiona was there though he could not make out her face only a blur and her long arms, the colour of the dress she'd been wearing that night. She was telling him again what he would do to his parents. The words were solid in the thick air; he watched them lifting from her mouth and coming towards him. She said them again and again more and more urgently each time, so that he felt he had missed something in the words, he had missed the meaning of them, their definition unclear. He reached out both hands towards her and she said – in Sarah's voice – *Margot?*

Sarah was sitting up with the blankets pulled around her, squinting at him through the steam off the cup she was drinking from. He was groggy, the room rearranging itself slowly around him.

Where's Gretel?

I took her up to the roof to sleep. She's fine, she's slept up there before. I needed a bit of sheesh.

He got up, stiff from lying on the hard floor. I'm sorry. I'll go up too. I'll sit with Gretel for a bit, he said.

She ignored him. Would you like some tea?

He was not sure if he nodded but she handed him a cup. Either side of her blanket he could see her shoulders were bare. At his feet there was a bundle of clothes. He raised the cup, missed his mouth, scalded his hand. From the bed he heard her soft laughter. Drank too fast, burned his tongue.

I think, he said—

Come here.

He found his feet moving. Like there was a current in the boat. It was still dark outside. She was naked beneath the blankets. His hands were shaking. She was undoing the buttons on his shirt, one by one. He felt a moment of quick unease that was the same, he thought, as forgetting a step, almost falling. She tugged at his socks and he wondered if it was better like this. Happening the way a natural disaster might, out of anyone's control. It was always, he thought, going to happen. This is why I came here. This is what I'm here for. And then: a wave of panic, beginning in his belly and climbing his throat. No, he thought, no. Fiona's face from the dream – a smooth shadowed blur of colour – swam into view, her mouth saying those awful words.

Hold on, he said. Put his hand on her shoulders.

Don't worry.

When she began to undo the buttons on his trousers he remembered suddenly what he had so easily forgotten. What was hidden.

Wait.

She shushed him, raising a hand, pulling the trousers down to his knees. It was cold on the boat but she was sweating. She pressed her face against his knees, drew in a breath. Seemed unsteady, hand over her mouth, face turned up towards him for a moment. I need, he said but she was moving fast, tugging the layers of tops over his head, reaching for skin. Pinching his belly between finger and thumb. He saw himself as she must do: the loops of cling film pulled tight across his chest, the strands of damp seaweed hair beneath his arms. Now her fingers were on the end of the cling film, turning him until it came loose. Her mouth like a cupped, wet hand over his nipple. That feeling again, as if the step had always been there and he, knowing, missed it purposefully, pitched down. She had tugged the underwear down before he could say anything. The mess of brown pubic hair, the seam that he could feel as if it were connected to the ends of his fingers, the tip of his tongue, the cords of his brain. She had turned away and was touching herself, grinding a hand between her legs, fingers on her breast. When she turned back it was almost forceful: his head knocking against the wall as they went down, one hand trapped at an angle beneath her weight, the smell of his breath in the air between them. She put her face between his legs and he could feel the sudden cool of her tongue. Realised then that she had known all along. The room tipped, tilted, drew in until he could feel the wall brushing the top of his face, the damp corners pushing inside him.

The Cottage

We should have stayed on the river; never come here. You are not made for houses. You are like an animal in a zoo, pacing the windows. I feel as if I am harming you, unintentionally. Like a child picking up an egg and accidentally crushing it. I wish I knew the way to do it. It has been nearly a month since I brought you back here on the bus, and I do not know how we will live this way for much longer. I try to run you a bath and you cringe away, crawl into the corner of the bathroom and weep.

It's OK, I say.

It's not OK, you say and then, Fuck.

All right.

Shit, you say. Shitting, bollocksing, pigging cock.

I laugh, and you look stunned in that way that babies do when they see something they've never seen before.

Frigging Jesus, I say.

You eye me, clutching the front of my bathrobe against your skinny chest. I take a breath.

Buggering, sodding, frigging, whoring poo.

You laugh once, almost a shout.

Gurning, barfing, shagging losers. I say, getting louder. I wait.

Tarts, you say.

Loony nuns, sons of bitches.

Tarts.

Bellends and knobs.

Farting priests, you say.

We are both laughing too hard to carry on. You're bent double with your fists pressed into your belly. I accidentally knock a bottle of shampoo off the edge of the bath, and that gets us both going again. When I straighten up and look at you you've stopped and are staring at me.

What are you laughing about? What's so funny? you say, and I feel a wave of seasick-like nausea sweeping over me. I tried to find you but instead found someone else who wears your face. You grunt.

Only joking, you say and laugh until you're crying. I put my arms around you. I put my arms around you and hold on as tightly as I can.

The next day you tell me you want to talk about the child you left behind.

It's fine, Mum, I say. I'm right here.

You are enraged. Not you. Not you.

In your notebook you draw a picture of a boat, faces in the square windows, the path running beside it like a road. You hold it up to show me. On the path there is a scrawled figure with her arms raised, holding the cylindrical shape of a wrapped child. I want to argue with you. I want to tell you that I don't want to hear stories about myself; I want to know about Marcus, about the Bonak. You are holding the drawing so tightly the edges bend. You have lost weight, mostly about the face. I try and remember if I am feeding you enough. I cannot remember the last time I ate or drank other than from the tap, cupping my hands. Your face is growing stormy, your hands balled.

OK, I say, OK. Whatever you want to tell me.

OK?

OK.

Sarah

You are thirty-three years old. You have new gravitational forces, new orbits: a child, a man. The words written in the dictionary of your mind are patience, selflessness. You smoke ten cigarettes a day. You dream of lakes big enough to hold planets.

When Charlie and the child were sleeping you sneaked out onto the path. There were no lights and the darkness was an object laid over everything. You stayed out until you were cold. Through the thin boat walls you heard the baby stirring, shifting; about to wake. There were sounds coming from further down. Something scrabbling, roughing the dirt. You pressed into the hedge. The sound came along the path and then onto the roof of the boat. When the child started to cry – not with much strength but persistently – you listened and so did the thing, still in the solid dark. You stood waiting for it to push its thick body down through the chimney, drop to the room below. The baby was in a crib at the foot of the bed where you slept. It would smell it out, nip a fold of blanket, carry it away with its clever claws. You wished it would happen before you could stop yourself. Naming a thing was powerful and silence was best. You pressed the wish back inside you and every day afterwards you thought, Now I will love her.

The child was ten months old but would not – despite Charlie's encouragement – learn to crawl. She liked sitting at the table, eating bananas or examining the picture books or jigsaws Charlie bought her from charity shops. She scooted on her bottom or rolled sideways, her legs flopping uselessly, never made it very far before coming to a rest again, seemingly contented.

What's that a picture of? Charlie would say, and she would look up as if stung, her face closed right in around itself. Come on, you can do it. Say da-dd-y. Say bo-a-t. How about mu-mm-y. Both of them swivelling to look at you. Say ri-v-er. Say swi-mm-ing.

In the morning she cried you awake and you always took a moment too long listening to her, the gusts of breathy panic, the small hands clenching and unfolding above her head. Charlie caught her in his arms, buried his face in her soft paunch. Looked up at you. Reproachful. Both of them. He did not understand. He loved her with such ease. When the child took your thumb in its hand and held it with that strange strength you wondered how you would ever be able to bear it.

It took you and Charlie nearly five months to come up with a name. He called her whatever took his fancy that week, names of birds he saw on the river – heron, moorhen, duckling – or words he liked the sound of. He called her Shush for a week and she eyed him curiously. One day he called her Gretel and it stuck. You said it to her quietly seeing if it would mean she somehow belonged, and she looked at you with those careful frown lines.

*

The creature you had wished into being was on the boat. You were uncertain of its shape and size only that there was a smell that had not been there before. Sometimes, sitting with the baby, you would look up and see her stiffening, a rut of hardness running across her small shoulders, eyes focusing on a space over your shoulder, spoon frozen halfway to her mouth. Or, out on the towpath, you'd catch her studying the boat, lip pushed forward, hands worrying away at the bottoms of her wet trousers. As if she could smell it, see it.

On one occasion you caught her sitting on the floor outside the bedroom, rolling marbles into the dark doorway, one after the other.

Who gave her marbles? I didn't give those to her.

For god's sake. Charlie jigged the baby up to his chest, pressed his face against her round cheeks. I gave them to her. What's wrong with you?

You wanted to tell him that what was wrong was that you'd made a wish and it had come true. You knew it without hesitation or question.

Charlie did not see, could not understand. In the evening, tired, sitting opposite you at the table, he said it was your Bonak.

You looked at him. What are you talking about? You were angry at him as well; a furious, white rage. How had he let this happen?

Your fear. Whatever it is you think you know. It's not real. It's not really there. It's boohooky, a conjuration, a shadow. It's a Bonak.

You didn't believe him but you nodded, took his hand. It was the first time you'd touched him in weeks. You're right. Yes. You're right. Laughing at the ridiculous word. It's a Bonak, nothing more than that. You let him take you into the bedroom, drawn into his orbit again, circling one another.

One night you could not sleep for the sound of the train. When you picked up the child and rested her on your hip she sat without complaint. You lifted her out of the boat and onto the path which was frosty. There were stones inside you, there were rocks. If you dropped into the water you would sink. There was half a moon, a crust, enough to see the great-bellied factories, the hill striding up to the town, her face as she looked at you. Don't worry, you said. She seemed heavier with every step you took.

At the end of the path, just beyond the bridge up to the road, some drunk kids had stolen a bin, left it on its side. You pulled out the last scraps of rubbish with your hands, told her to hold out her arms and threaded them through the jumpers you had brought. She looked at you from between the slats of her fingers the way Charlie sometimes did when he was playing.

Don't worry. You placed her into the bin; peeled her an orange and gave it to her, told her a couple of Charlie's riddles until she seemed to sleep.

You walked away back up the path. It was darker than it had been, and the factories were hidden, the sludge of water, the blocks of same-faced houses. You walked until the light started coming over the square roofs, across the greasy water, through the grid of the railway bridges. You walked and walked. You walked right out of the town and you kept on going until there were blisters on your feet. The realisation of what you'd done came slowly over the next couple of days. You could barely conceive of yourself as a person who would do such a thing. You could see her small hands, face turned up and serious in thought; her chubby legs drawn up to her chest. You had left her. You had left your child behind.

The year was 1983 and two men are in space for 211 days, the longest anyone has ever spent there. You understood how they feel. You had washed up in another rental room. Worked a couple of days a week in a grocer's, filling other people's shopping bags. Told yourself and anyone who asked that you didn't miss him, that whittling-handed boatman who'd taught you to smoke and cook. You didn't miss him. You didn't miss him until you did.

To your surprise – after everything that had happened – you were no longer land-loving. It made you nervous: the sturdiness of concrete and fence posts, pavements, car parks. You felt wary around stairs, cellars, corridors. Found yourself awake in the middle of the night, damp, the room rocking on a current that was not there, your feet freezing with a cold slipstream of river. Found yourself hanging around boatyards, lusting after the shiny tourist crafts decked out with stoves, four-door ovens, beds that fell out of the wall. You could not afford anything like that. You did not know who could. But, at a push, you could buy the junker out the back of the yard that was soon to be taken apart for scrap.

You drove it as far as it would go before the engine burned out. You liked the place you had landed. The river had a strong flow littered with debris which you watched flashing past. There was a muddy stretch you imagined – though you never would – planting with vegetables. Beyond there were trees. No one else was around.

There must have been – at some point – another man. A boatman, passing by, on his way somewhere else and dropped in for the night. It has never mattered who it was.

You never left space for it to matter. There was a man and, after a time, there was me. Nothing much yet, barely a thought.

By the time you realised you were pregnant it was too late to do anything about it. Towards the tail ends of the nights you were kept awake by thoughts of what you would do when the baby came, how you would manage when you had done so badly before. It was, you thought, penance. You thought that hell might be living the same days over and over, stuck in a wedge of time, unable to shake yourself loose.

I was born in the spring. In my mind it is the same as every spring I'd ever spent in that place. The nights were cold but cut off earlier; the ground was peppered with what might be, with what could come. You were cooking with your sleeves rolled up. You shouted my name and it twangs forward through the ancient years, bruising as it comes, tinged with just-born blood. A second-hand name, a name that would always make you think of someone else. Gretel, you called me. Gretel.

You strapped me to the front of your chest, put your hair up in a scarf and scrubbed away rust and dirt until your hands were rough as the trunks of the pines that grew not far from the bank. You did not bother fixing the engine but mended the broken doors and the roof hatch. There was no one but you and me. I was not the same as that lost baby. Every day you were reminded of it. I pointed at everything I could see. Tree, I said. Tree. Boat. Water. I ran as soon as I could walk. I loved talking and writing words down. I read every book you could get your hands on. When you found an old Scrabble board I sat for hours arranging the tiles into longer and longer words. You gave me a bunch of wire to play with, and when you looked back I had made some strange contraption, a wind chime that sang in the breeze.

Occasionally you thought of that other lost child. Counted her birthdays. Tried to keep her in your head. The way she would – the time she had – remember when. Except hour by hour it was harder to do. She was carried away and one morning you woke and you could not even remember what her face had looked like. Days went on, years twisted past. Memory had a habit of erasing, leaving only the most necessary. You stood on the roof rolling a cigarette you put in your mouth but did not smoke. It was winter again. The river was high, restless.

The River

Sarah, Marcus and Gretel took shifts watching. It was impossible not to see the Bonak in every tree branch carried by the current, in the water that flushed from the weir or hurried against the sides of the boat. It had been winding its way through the shallows, pushing into the thick bushes on either side of the locks, clambering in the places more rock than water. It had been coming, he thought, like something they had half-forgotten. Like something they should have known. He thought of Sarah's hands, lined, red from the hot water, the way his skin had turned white beneath the pressure of her fingers. He thought of his parents, who were – though he wasn't to know this – still hunting for him, replacing the posters of his face after the heavy rains, not sleeping. He thought of the things Fiona had told him he would do. When Sarah took over he slept in the pile of blankets. Threading through his dreams was the Bonak, barely moving. Sarah rode on its back, bare knees tucked together. When it grew too shallow to swim she strung it around her neck, walked forward over the stones. Its mouth was ajar and hidden inside was a truth he had not found yet, something he was supposed to know. He pressed his hands inside its mouth, and the jaws closed like a vice around his wrists.

He dozed on his watch, rising out of sleep, marched the length of the boat to keep himself awake, slapping his cheeks until his face hurt, biting down on his tongue. The fog around the trees had spread. He went back inside for bread and they stopped talking, looked at him as if he was a stranger. He ate it fast, sat on the cold roof. The ache between his legs was gone, as if it had never been there. The blood moving around his body seemed slow, barely reaching the extremities. He watched as it started to get light. He began to imagine what he would do when they had found the Bonak, where he would go. There would be another journey, another long walk. He did not think he minded.

From the cage there was the noise of the gate falling. He waited for Sarah to come up from inside the boat but she did not – had not, he thought, heard. She was asleep perhaps. Both of them. He did not want her to come. He wanted her to be safe. He stumbled forward to the edge of the roof, tried to see into the cage. Could not. Lowered himself off the edge of the boat and onto the wooden runnel that ran around the sides. He would go into the water; he would swim to the bank and see what was in the cage. He would do this so she would not have to. He would do this because he had left his parents behind and he was no longer certain that had been the right thing to do. He was close enough to the water to feel the ice of it, like a secondary pulse through his ankles. He dropped down. His head dipped beneath the surface, mouth filled. He quickly lost the direction of the air, the direction he had come from. When he came out the current had already carried him a fair distance, the cage no longer straight ahead but behind him.

He kicked hard against the drag, bad leg angling out of the water, doing no good. At times he felt something willowing past him but it was always only leaves, yellow foam, a plastic bag that caught on one foot and then was carried away. The water was icy. A branch was carried against him, almost took him with it. Another looked so like the Bonak that he went under, flailing. The water tasted of mud and oil, of yeast. Fiona was there with him, the tendrils of her long, thin hair. She could control the weather, baked cakes no one wanted to eat, knew what was coming before it came. She lay on the bottom of the river and drank until the water was gone. You will kill your father, she said when she had enough breath. You will have sex with your mother.

He came up, kicked out. The bank was nearer, and he felt beneath his feet the ground beginning. He'd left, that's what he'd done. He'd left so he wouldn't do the things Fiona said he would do. His hands suddenly felt so full he could not close them. They were full as they lifted the body of the dead man and let him go into the water; they were full with Sarah's face, with her feet, which he'd held.

It was colder out of the water than in. His clothes were heavy. At the base of the pines the fog made the trunks of the trees footless. The rocks were slippery near the bank and a thick reed sliced across a cheek so that he watched the water he was wading through turn, momentarily, red. Gretel could have told him the word for knowing the truth of something after it was too late; all he knew was that he should have taken his boots off before he went in. He pulled at one, watched the water sluicing from it. He could feel all the nerves in his jaw, tight as a cord strung between trees. He had killed Charlie. He'd had sex with Sarah.

He moved along the bank towards the cage. It was set close to the water and he came around behind it. His teeth juddered in his mouth. It was quiet, and he wondered if he had made a mistake. He went forward on all fours. He was very close to the cage now, the insides hidden by the grasses they had dragged over it. From the tops of the trees something called and called. He moved aside the tangle of branches. He expected to see it. It was beyond imagination; it would break out through the cage towards him.

Except there was nothing inside. The cage door had fallen shut on its own. He went around and braced his body against the door, trying to heave it open and back into place so that the mechanism could reset. The river slipped past just behind him. The mud was soft; his feet sank in. He pushed harder at the rim of the cage door with his arms, felt it starting to lift.

There was a sound from the boat. When he looked back the barge seemed about ready to break away, side on to the current, the mooring ropes straining by his feet. Sarah had come out onto the roof and was watching him. He could not see her face in the dim light. Her body looked like a blade in the darkness.

The edge of the door slipped from his hands, banged closed once more. He left it, tried to turn to see Sarah better, perhaps to say something to her. What would he say? Just in front of him the river ran fast and freely. The bank was uneven, pitted with holes. The mud caught at his foot and he stumbled, fell away from the cage and into the water. He dropped hard into the flow of the river.

The current caught him immediately and carried him down and away from the bank and the trap. The water tasted the way she had done; fingers to the knuckle in his mouth. He closed his eyes but when he opened them there was no difference. He kicked out, tried to push upwards. He waited for her to come. She had seen him falling. She would come for him. The air passing from her lungs into his, her cold mouth open against his cold mouth. She would save him because she was his mother. He struck out one-legged, grinding upwards, nearly there. Except where he'd expected to break through there was only more water. The air bubbled out and was gone. He opened his eyes wide, looking for the white-star explosion of her body hitting the water. River debris – carried for miles with the current, connected with his ribs, pressed him along. More came with force against his face, and he felt a blinding mess of pain across his eyes before the cold took it away. The darkness was comfortable. He tested it with his hands. She was not coming. He was waiting for her. The river dug him down, held him under.

The current took him quickly in its arms and carried him along and away from the place by the pines. The river was called the Isis and it had carried bodies before, all the way to the Thames and on and afterwards to the sea. There was snowmelt and heavy rain, and the water carried him fast, tumbling along, now face down, now looking up towards the shards of light-broken surface. Through cities and stuck at tree-dredged weirs and then on once more. And someone might have found him. Fishermen sitting out in the cold waiting for pulls on their lines. Or commuters paused on a quiet bridge for a cigarette. Might have found him and dragged him out and called the police, who would find, eventually, Roger and Laura, who'd been waiting for just that call and would have gone to the morgue I had once gone to looking for you. And it would have changed everything or nothing.

Except no one did find him. The river carried him as far as it wanted and then buried him.

The Hunt

On the river I sat with you beside the fire.

I'm hungry, you said.

A memory is bothering me. The memory of the meal with Fiona had come right to the front of my brain like a stranger to a kitchen window and was tapping.

Did you hear me? I'm hungry.

We'll go soon, I said. Do you want to? I have a cottage on a hill. I think you'd like it.

You looked at me as if I was mad. We can't leave him, you said. We can't leave him here alone.

I left you beside the fire and walked into the trees. I could smell the Chinese food, could hear the sound of Fiona's fork scraping the bottom of the plates, the chef in the kitchen having an argument with someone on the phone. Towards the end of telling the story Fiona paused and sat back with her fists resting high on her ribs. Looked at me. Better, she said, to let it die out. Better to let it die out here. But I'd only sat and waited until she shrugged, rocked forward, began to tell me what had happened the night of Roger's birthday. The smell of the candles on the cake Fiona made that did not rise. The spring rolls that came with the takeaway and were not crispy enough. Everyone a little drunk, empty wine bottles in the recycling bin, bits of cheese cut haphazardly off the block in the fridge. I saw Margot at the sink with her back to the room. She was wearing yellow washing-up gloves and her long hair was tied up away from her soft, lovely face. She had your eyes. Of course she did. She had my eyes. Behind her Fiona started to talk. She said: you will kill your father. You will have sex with your mother.

I crouched in the forest and buried my hands in the pine needles. My tongue was thick in my throat, and when I tried to shout to you nothing came. I could feel the words dropping away from me as easily as they were dropping away from you. I could see Margot in the kitchen of the house. She looked over Fiona's shoulder at me. She was a ghost. I could feel her haunted hands on my face and arms. She had believed that Laura and Roger were her parents and she had left to protect them. I could feel her breath in my mouth, her fist moving inside my open hand. Except they were not her parents. I put my head down onto the ground. I could hear you chattering away by the fire, occasionally pausing as if listening, occasionally laughing in a way I did not recognise. The dizziness retreated like a flat bank of fog. The earth smelled damp, like rotting mushrooms. With my hands flat to it I was certain I could feel the mulch underneath of insects and growing roots. I sat back. From the scrub you were silent. I needed to get you back to the cottage, where there was food and water and a bed. I needed to decide what to do with you, to decide what to do with myself. I stood up and turned. There was something silhouetted between the thin pines. I held up a hand to shade my eyes, and at the motion it broke forward and came fast across the flat ground, pumping its thick legs and with its head raised from the neck and its tail slicing back and forth across the ground. I stepped back and lost my footing. It came fast, and I knew then that it meant to kill me and keep you on the river, and then – from nowhere – you were there, waving the spade above your head, screaming some kind of war cry and lunging at it so that the Bonak – because it was the Bonak – changed direction at the last moment and went streaking away through the trees, you following after, and was gone.

I ran after you. It seemed colder – the way it was that winter – the ground very hard beneath my boots. I thought I saw Marcus shifting between the trees. I had lost you. I ran until I hit the mesh fence, beyond which was a railway track dug into the earth, and then circled back to the scrub. You were not there. I did not understand how you could have run so fast. I moved again into the trees. Shouted and shouted. Thought I heard an answering echo. The pines dropped back and so did the land. I heard the river before I saw it. You were down by the water, bent over, facing away from me, back hunched. The ground around you was sodden and the water was rust coloured. I felt my feet starting to move from under me. The spade I'd used to break into the boat was by your side. The metal was wet with blood. The river was safe for the first time in decades. I imagined that he did not fight, that he felt as if – after all this time – he knew you. And you had done it for me. I moved down the bank. You were stripping the rough, scaly hide away from the flesh, tugging it free. Its legs were short and strong, clawed; its mouth was long and toothy, its tail vanished into the murky water, its body was thick and rough until the belly, which was pale as churned cream. You were up to your arms in Bonak. I watched you and – for a moment – it seemed as if you were turning into it. As if you had been it all along.

It took me a long time to dig the hole. My arms were weedy from desk work, my heart thundered. You had skinned it and were by the water washing the hide clean, scraping at it the way you used to do with the carcasses we would get off the butcher's boat. When I cut into it there were organs, blood, muscle so tough my knife could barely get through. I finished the hole. It was starting to get dark in that way it did in summer, gradually, sneaking up. A loon called and – down by the water – you called back. I built the fire until it boomed into the sky. The forest seemed to give up everything I needed, as if it had been waiting for this moment. The fire shouted higher than my head. You came up and sat beside it, holding your hands out to warm them. You had the Bonak hide thrown around your shoulders, its mouth resting on your head, its limbs wrapped around you. You looked hybrid, scabby knees protruding, tufts of white hair like strange fur beneath the Bonak's slack jaws. I cut slabs of meat from the carcass, skewered them, watched them blacken. We took turns holding each of the organs, weighing them with the same kind of wonder with which we used to the read the encyclopedia. The brain was small, bluish; the lungs were enormous; the liver was bigger than the heart but the heart was so strong I couldn't pierce it. I pushed it into the ash at the centre of the fire.

We ate with our fingers. It reminded me of the feasts we would have on the boat, when the butcher came round or someone passing dropped off new food, squashes or sweet peppers, bread and goats' cheese. It reminded me of eating in the restaurant with Fiona, scoffing, eating too much as if to make up for the story coming out of her. There was jubilation in food and there was apology, forgiveness. The meat was gamey, a little like the fish we used to eat from the water. The blood ran down my wrists. The dark lowered in. I prodded the fire to life. Dug the heart out with a stick.

Eight

Beginnings

The Cottage

The craggy shape of you in the armchair, your head tipped back, your arms laid out along the rests. The rain battering down outside the windows and flooding the field. You will eat only oranges, which I peel for you by the dozen. When I bring you glasses of water you empty them onto the floor. Marcus speaks through your mouth or I do. I watch you walking down a narrow towpath with a child in your arms that is not me but that has my name. Through the glass hatch of the boat I watch bodies rubbed together like coins, repeating and repeating. The floor of the sitting room grows rough like the river, and beneath the surface there are bodies, mine or Marcus's, twisting in a current that carries them away.

I am so angry at you I can barely see. I rage and you sit quietly or rage with me, slamming the kitchen door, knocking things off the table. I think of all the ways I could punish you. Withholding food, keeping you awake, opening the door and simply letting you wander away. When you cry you put your arms around my neck and cling on. You are not yourself. You are not the person who did any of those things. You do not remember the language that made you that person. You hold your wrinkled face hard against mine, your hands scrabbling at my clothes to hold me closer. When you clap your hands the roof hatch appears between them, fizzing light into my dark sitting room.

Some mornings I am cold with certainty that only some ancient punishment will do, a stoning or a blinding, leaving you out for the wolves. You tell me that you didn't know and we grow silent and wonder if either of us really believes that. Again and again I go back to the idea that our thoughts and actions are determined by the language that lives in our minds. That perhaps nothing could have happened except that which did. Effing along, sheesh time, harpiedoodle, sprung, messin, Bonak. Bonak, Bonak, Bonak. Words like breadcrumbs. As if all along *Bonak* didn't mean what we were afraid of, what was in the water, but watch out; this is what is coming down the river.

It is over a month since I brought you back. We come to a stalemate and do not speak at all. Move around one another in strict circles of ownership: the sitting room is yours, I take the bedroom and the kitchen; the bath belongs to you. Talking would mean that we would have to discuss it and we will not do that. What you did. What happened when you had Margot. I make fish fingers and leave them beside your chair when you are in your bath. One day I find a half-eaten bar of chocolate on my pillow. Another day you break all the bowls in the cupboard, and I go outside into the rain and get on a bus and go into town and wander around the shops. Stand in the doorways to wait out the strong swells of storm. Find myself in the supermarket we'd gone to that time. I am certain that when I get back you will be gone and I am not sure how I feel about that. Except you are not gone. Where would you go? I make you dinner. You have forgotten our fight and you touch my hair and hands, tell me that you like the rain, don't I?

The next day I watch the words leaving you. The pronouns are slippery and won't stay still; objects go first so that you only point or shout until I bring what you want. Names are long gone. Some days you talk about children you once had, but when I ask what they were called you cannot or will not reply. We play small games, time-fillers which you do with such intense concentration it gives me headaches to watch you. Left and right, up and down. What's this called? What time is it? What year is it? I wait for the stories to leave you. It would be best for them to go. Everything you told me. But they stick around, come surging out of you again and again, your hands clamped over your mouth to try and hold them back. The house is filled with everything that went on. Marcus's cold face is up against the rain-streaked windows, looking out of the mirror when I brush my teeth, standing beside your armchair. The Bonak is here too, rattling through the rooms above our heads, languishing in the bath. Now and then it has your eyes or long feet rather than a tail. Now and then it has fur rather than scales or walks upright or is a shadow, barely even there. The river curls through the corner of the sitting room, upsets the floorboards. Trees break through the wet plaster and lay their roots around us. There is – in the night – the sound of the train. There are flat-roofed boats floundering and a man who whittles a lure big enough to catch what we are afraid of. Whatever we are afraid of.

Don't, I tell you when you start speaking. You don't have to any more.

But the telling is involuntary and won't stop even when I slip sleeping tablets into your tea or try and distract you with old black and white films on my laptop or talk to you about the history of lexicography or spread jigsaws on the floor for you. Your mouth gapes open and they repeat and repeat.

The next day when I come downstairs you've unplugged the fridge and taken everything from the freezer and out of its packets and spread it across the floor. To begin with I am calm. We make a game of gathering the scattered fish fingers, vegetarian sausages, spring rolls and balls of spinach. I tell you we'll have a feast like the old days, and you smile, follow me doggedly when I go to turn the oven on, help me lay out sheets of foil. I am taken by the sudden simplicity of it and tell you that we'll bake a cake for pudding. I go to the cupboard to get out ingredients and when I turn back you have both arms to the elbow in the hot oven. I shout and you fall backwards towards me. The skin on your arms is red and blistering already, around the knuckles. I drag you to the sink and turn the cold water on. You don't make a sound.

What were you doing? What were you thinking? I realise that I am shouting, your burned arms clenched in my hands, and that you are staring at me with your mouth open. I let you go and you scuttle away into the sitting room. I turn off the oven and go upstairs and lie on the bed, listen to the battering of the rain, close my eyes. By the time I come downstairs you have forgotten what happened and are standing over my desk, looking down at the index cards, as if halfway through a task you mean to finish. I find cream in the bathroom and put it on the burns. You watch with such concentration that I clear my throat, chat meaninglessly to try and distract you.

Did I do that? you say.

Yes. But it doesn't matter.

After what happens with the oven there are other occasions when you hurt yourself. At first they are – or seem – accidental, only another consequence of your being ill. You pick at the old burns until they bleed, try to run yourself a bath and forget to put in cold, trip down the last few stairs and crack your knee on the tiles. You go again and again to the oven and try to turn on the grill or press your hands inside.

What are you doing?

Seeing if it's hot enough.

Well, stop please.

You develop a cold fascination with the knives in the cutlery drawer, the sharp edges of tables, electricity sockets and the toaster. I fill the cellar with everything I can think could cause you harm and you hunt for them the way you once did alcohol. You do not know the names for objects but you know which ones you want, jabber and grab at me, anguished and downright pissed off. You stop eating.

I do not see it for what it is until I go to the bathroom one day and – coming back downstairs – catch you with your head in a sink full of cold water, the surface pocked with air and you gripping both sides of the basin to hold yourself down. I heave you up.

What are you doing? What are you doing?

You won't answer, glare at me sullenly. I wrap your head in the tea towel and rub harder than necessary until you come up red-eyed and damp-headed, looking at me.

I would like, you say with the most clearness you've had for days, to forget now.

I pack up the pills from the medicine cabinet, the bleach from under the sink, matches, razors, scissors, glass. I turn off the electricity and the water. The cellar has no lock so I make you come with me as I carry everything down to the bin at the bottom of the track. You refuse to wear the hood; the rain streaks your hair and face. I cannot tell from the way you look at me if you understand what I'm doing.

You'll forget anyway, I tell you. Though of this I am not so sure. My name and your own, the names of objects in the house, numbers, days of the week, light and dark, night and day: all – at one time or another – you seem to forget. But the story of Margot and the man who was her father, the story of the Bonak and where it came from, these you do not forget for even one moment.

We walk back up the hill. The mud splatters the backs of our legs. I hold your hand and you, mutely, let me.

Days of near terror. Catching you at the top of the stairs about to throw yourself down. Stopping you from scraping open your wrists on anything you can find. There is a coolness to the way you go about it. A degree of serenity which scares me more than anything else. You seem quietly impatient whenever I catch you. You call me by name and let yourself be moved away without resistance. You seem to know more; know where you are and how you got there. You tell me shards and fragments of the past over and over, like echoes. Stop, I tell you, but you do not seem able. I do not sleep because you wait until I do and then climb the stairs and go to the windows, try to open them. I think of calling someone but it feels like a betrayal. You never would have called anyone for help. I tie you to me with a length of cord and we pull one way and then the other. I make you eat. You wail and then are quiet. The words spill out of you. You speak in phrases that do not seem your own, heavy with meaning. You tell me that you are the start of everything that has happened. You tell me your blood is the root and that you want to forget. I do not know what to reply.

The rain gets worse. The road at the bottom of the hill floods, and when I lift the telephone there isn't even a dial tone. Out of the window we can see that the stream has become a deluge, threshing across the muddy ground, deep, perhaps, as that old river where I found you. You are sick from something you eat. I hold your thin hair back from your damp face. There is the noise of water on the roof and on the hill. We doze on the floor. I dream that you are gone and I am in a different house. There are other people there but their faces are grey and shiny like seal skin, and I cannot make them out. In the dream I had never found you, did not know you, was motherless in a quiet, resigned way. In the dream I knew nothing but the everyday: how to wash dishes or iron the creases out of clothes, how to drive a car and post a letter. I slept through the nights, went out for breakfast at the weekends or took a car that belonged to me and went walking. There was a dog that looked like an otter and could hold its breath under the water.

I have slept and left you on your own. The door of the bathroom is open wide. I shout for you. I cannot find you. I shout your name. I know what has happened. I run through the rooms. I phone for an ambulance though I have not yet found you. I tell them the address and put the phone down. I shout and look and cannot find you. I run outside. The rain has withdrawn and there is sun on the puddles and on the dirty front of the house and on your face. You have taken the sheet from your bed and hanged yourself from the window.

I cut you down. Death has worn you smooth as a stone. I hold my hands to the side of your face, the top of your head, your ankles, your shoulders, your wrists. I want – sitting there, clinging onto your body – to say something. To end the story. To finish what we started. But, though I stay with you for a long time, no words come to me. Eventually I will get up and open the doors and windows of the house to dry it out.

The Cottage

The places we are born come back to us. They disguise themselves as words, memory loss, nightmares. They are the way we sometimes wake with a pressure on our chests that is animal-like or turn on a light and see someone we'd thought was long gone standing there looking at us. It's winter again. The heating clanks and clangs in the mornings, and there is frost on the wrong side of the windows. When I walk up to the spring it is frozen. The radio stations are filled with car crashes, delayed trains. This year I miss winters on the river. The silence. No one but you. I keep waiting for you to come back. If anyone would return to haunt me it would be you. But the house is still, and if you are there you aren't talking. The thought that there will be winters and winters for ever is inconceivable. You are dead and have taken with you more than a decade of bad feeling, a swamp of miscommunication, missed birthdays, the whole of my twenties, a cut-away breast I was not there to witness going and Margot and everything that happened to her. I think often of all the dead who live in the water.

I understand that I must move on. I return to the office, work at my desk. Go for tentative drinks with the other lexicographers in a pub called the Fox and Hound. I wish the dog was here. Think about rescuing one. Do nothing about it. There are more good days than bad. I do not, yet, ask for more. On the bad days I remember how on the river everything's sinking, the half-bodied shape of the locks beneath the scum, the intestines of roots and trees. And I know that further upstream it grows narrow as a corkscrew; that there is a yellowing of foam along the banks and a heron stands in the chug of weir as if he's waiting for something.

Acknowledgements

About a year into writing this book my partner made me a little framed sign for my desk. The sign was one that I had written but rarely believed. It said: I think this book is going to be really fucking good. Daisy Johnson. The sign serves, now, as a reminder that it is impossible to write a book alone. I could not have written this one without the following:

Amelie Chanarin, who I hope will one day read this book with the knowledge that much of it was edited while she napped.

Susie and Martin Bradshaw and Emma George, without whom this book would not exist.

Alex Bowler, who said yes to this book right at the beginning.

Steve, Fiona and everyone else at Graywolf.

Everyone at Jonathan Cape for all their hard work. Particular thanks to Ana, Clare, Michal, Joe, Nick and Suzanne.

Chris Wellbelove and everyone else at Aitken Alexander.

Jack Ramm, who worked, and I suspect despaired over, this book nearly as much as I did.

To the people sat across the table: Jessie, Jess, Laura and Hannah.

Because nothing would ever get written without them: Sarvat, Kiran and Tom.

To Matt of the aforementioned sign. May there be van trips, always.

To Big Jake. To Pollyanna and Jake. To my Grandmother.

To my parents, for whom I do all my writing.

To the booksellers and the bookshops. Most particularly Blackwell's Oxford.

To everyone who read and recommended *Fen* to their friends and families. To everyone who will read and, fingers crossed, recommend this book.

penguin.co.uk/vintage